Hoppla!
1 2 3

Originally published in French as *Hop là ! un deux trois* by P.O.L. éditeur, 2001

Library of Congress Cataloging-in-Publication Data

Gavarry, Gérard.
[Hop là!, un, deux, trois. English]
Hoppla! 1 2 3 / Gerard Gavarry ; translated by Jane Kuntz. -- 1st English translation.
   p. cm.
ISBN 978-1-56478-536-7 (pbk. : alk. paper)
  1. Teenage boys--France--Fiction. 2. Poor teenagers--France--Fiction. 3. Murder-
-France--Fiction. 4. Alienation (Social psychology)--Fiction. 5. Violence--Social
aspects--Fiction. 6. Juvenile delinquency--Social aspects--Fiction. I. Kuntz, Jane. II.
Title. III. Title: Hoppla! one, two, three.
  PQ2667.A97474H6613 2009
  843'.914--dc22

                    2008050087

Partially funded by grants from the National Endowment for the Arts, a federal
agency; the Illinois Arts Council, a state agency; and by the University of Illinois at
Urbana-Champaign.

Cet ouvrage, publié dans le cadre d'un programme d'aide à la publication, bénéficie du
soutien du Ministère des Affaires étrangères et du Service Culturel de l'Ambassade de
France aux Etats-Unis.

This work, published as part of the program of aid for publication, received support
from the French Ministry of Foreign Affairs and the Cultural Services of the French
Embassy in the United States.

www.dalkeyarchive.com

Cover: design by Danielle Dutton, illustration by Nicholas Motte

Printed on permanent/durable acid-free paper and bound in the
United States of America

Hoppla! 1 2 3

GÉRARD GAVARRY

TRANSLATED BY JANE KUNTZ

Dalkey Archive Press
Champaign and London

Und an diesem Mittag wird es still sein am Hafen
Wenn man fragt, wer wohl sterben muß.
Und dann werden Sie mich sagen hören: Alle!
Und wenn dann der Kopf fällt, sag ich: Hoppla!

In that noonday heat there'll be a hush round the harbor
As they ask which has got to die.
And you'll hear me as I softly answer: the lot!
And as the first head rolls I'll say: hoppla!

Bertolt Brecht
The Threepenny Opera

1. The Coconut Palm

1.01

Radio messages were streaming into Traffic Watch Central, growing more alarmist as rush hour loomed, gradually drowning out the electronic buzz that sent a continuous shiver through the control room. To file their reports, far-flung correspondents would repeat the name of their town or locality as if they themselves were Rocquencourt, or Joinville-le-Pont, Paris-Campagne, or Pompadour. Voices also beamed in from helicopters, signing on with such aerial code names as *Dragonfly*, *Echinargus Nab*, or *Mouchka 2000*, while others, earthbound, sputtered twice in crackly rapid-fire "Car T100 to TWC" or "P 050 here, P 050, do you read me? Over."

"TWC here," a man or woman would answer, one of thirteen controllers on duty, each seated in front of a screen, a keyboard, a mike, and all facing the thirty-square-meter map of Île-de-France at one twenty-thousandth scale.

In the course of these transmissions, tiny points of light moved about the gigantic map, blinking on and off in a rolling *trompe l'oeil* wherever traffic was flowing smoothly, but elsewhere barely twinkling, or already clustered into large patches, growing at the same rate and in the same proportions as their counterparts on the real network of streets, they would enlarge, stretch, and, incidentally, retract before resuming their entropic dispersal across the map; so that eventually, having been halted by a succession of stop signs and tricolor traffic lights, the automobile population in motion reached its maximum density on the highways out of Paris into the suburbs, by which time the entire map of Île-de-France was aglow with glittering trails of luminescence: elegantly arched trajectories, some weirdly sinusoidal, other sections impeccably straight, these being the most numerous, a jumble looking like the ruins of some immense multi-columned piece of architecture.

Movement did sometimes occur in this petrified landscape. A daredevil driver, exasperated by all the delays, would tear out of his lane onto the shoulder and, in flagrant violation of the law, pass everyone on the right. Elsewhere, on one of the superhighways, a few cars in tight formation were driving at top speed, destination Paris, while in the other direction all four lanes were gridlocked. At TWC, this would appear—depending on the circumstances—as a raised dot, climbing, like some kind of lizard, or else as an oval of light in freefall, like a ripe fruit, heavy with its sudden, overwhelming attraction to the ground. Or, if vehicles began pulling away from an intersection, gradually communicating themselves into various converging lanes, the remote transmission converted this movement into an undulation that, when repeated often enough, registered on the giant map as a gracefully nimble rocking motion, as if caused by a breeze off the open sea. While responding to the umpteenth radio call, the controllers thought they could hear the steady sound of surf, the rubbing and sucking of the undertow. The more imaginative among them could feel a warm breeze on their skin. And in the control room's artificial light, faces grew dreamy, just as bodies—sitting only minutes before in hunched and tense positions at the foot of Île-de-France—now felt weightless, supple, relaxed, as though relieved of their own gravity, spared any aches or fatigue.

An accident brought this fantasy to a rude halt.

"Location?" asked TWC.

A voice in the headset replied: "National Seven, Orly, passage under the South Terminal."

"Category?"

"Five-zero J five-five," said the voice, which in laymen's terms meant that a tractor-trailer had caught fire and that the road wouldn't be clear for another forty-five minutes.

Attempts were being made to cordon off the now-impassable portion of the road. For several kilometers upstream, and as many downstream, mobile barricades prohibited any new access to the underground passage. Already, the giant electronic panels that spanned the N7 or the A108 highways at regular intervals between Villejuif and Corbeil-Essonnes were displaying the word ACCIDENT in brightly lit letters, and most of the access roads along the way had now become detours. This resulted in an anarchic swarm of automobiles filling up the entire local grid. Migratory flows intermixed, intertwined, increased, and multiplied, becoming long processions, wandering in slow motion, searching in the dusk for some alternate route. A cold rain began to fall, soaking the gray of the sky, the red of the brake lights, the white, yellow, and orange of headlights and suburban glare. Car hoods were steaming. Windows were streaming. Behind every windshield, the blurred, wavy image of the driver concealed the same fool's fantasy: that the cars in front were going to suddenly vanish in a flash! . . . Or that the road would grow wider, they'd start moving again, pick up speed; or at very least, that they could slip into third gear and take their left foot off the shift pedal for a while.

And yet, by the thousands, car radios were making it clear that none of this was going to happen any time soon. The broadcasters counseled patience, sympathized: "Well, it looks like a real mess out there in the south suburbs." They played sunny, cheerful music to stave off the aggravation, the boredom, the inertia that sets in after a day on the job exacerbated by a traffic jam. Or via the husky voice of some female announcer, they endeavored to lull drivers into believing that the eternal feminine itself had infused the enclosed, dry, and, on the whole, cozy interior spaces of each of their vehicles: "You're furious out there on the N7, aren't you?" simpered one, or more often two, even four car radio speakers—for example. Or, "Looks like there's no way you'll be catching that plane," and "Now, don't you wish you'd moved to Futuna . . . ?" But all these words, from *looks like* to *Futuna*, went unheard by Madame Fenerolo, and no less so by her passenger, the former having with one finger peremptorily pressed the OFF button after *you're furious*.

1. 02

As quickly as a set change between scenes, all the stray shopping carts in the parking lot were gathered up, stacked together under the awning, and chained to the iron grate pulled down in front of the entrances to the SUMABA. By then, the parking lot was practically empty, except for the store-owned vans lined up along the western fence, and, about fifty meters away, the gray Opel belonging to the manager, Madame Fenerolo. She was already walking toward her car when she stopped in her tracks and wheeled around to proffer some final advice to the security guards. She is gesticulating as she speaks, pointing her car keys toward the shopping carts that have to be put somewhere else, or turned in the other direction, or more securely fastened. Standing next to the Opel, Bessie waits. The other cashiers have already left, but not Bessie, resident of Ris-Orangis, as is Madame Fenerolo, who is giving her a ride home. The tall silhouettes of the streetlamps planted in staggered rows in front of Bessie, the patch of orange mist they hold suspended above the blacktop, make the parking lot look all the more deserted, flat and submerged in darkness, while on the horizon, well beyond the vans, clouds swell with a last pale hint of twilight. Bessie gazes in that direction. She's neither humming nor moving, but simply adjusting her focus on the infinite, the way our eyes do before a seascape—night falls, the air is still, the coconut palms rise all the way to the beach, and we wonder, seeing them thus against the light, whether they might once have been human beings, contemplators of the vastness, sentinels of the millennia, fathomers of the abyss . . . And we yearn to join in their immobile ballet, at the risk of falling under the same spell that first turned them into coconut palms.

"You'd never know the days were getting longer," says Madame Fenerolo.

And again she says: "I'm going by way of Fontenay, there's less traffic than on the N20," and then, "I like your new cardigan. Where'd you get it?"

She applies her thumb mindlessly to her keychain to unlock the car doors. She'll already have taken the Fontenay road before declaring, again, "I'm taking the Fontenay road." And without waiting for an answer to her question about the cardigan, she'll have segued into, "We might be opening a seafood department. That'd be nice, wouldn't it, a seafood department?"

"Yes, that'd be nice," Bessie concedes.

They've passed Croix de Berny. Traffic has slowed down considerably. Between Fresnes Prison and the next highway interchange, Madame Fenerolo leans on her steering wheel and, pressing a finger against the windshield, she points to a large apartment building.

"I almost moved to this area. It was a house right behind the big building there."

Bessie cranes her neck, indifferent, while mumbling something like "uh huh" or "um hum." Because of the proximity of the prison, she doesn't quite understand which building is referred to. Madame Fenerolo has no regrets—obviously, Fresnes would have been closer to the SUMABA than Ris-Orangis, but she likes Ris, and Bessie does too, doesn't she . . . She starts another sentence—"The trouble with," or "What's good about"— which she interrupts to listen to the dirge on the car radio.

"Oh no . . . !"

From Fresnes, heading south, the A106 and N7 are momentarily inaccessible.

And: tomorrow, like today, Île-de-France will shiver, cough, sneeze, and ache all over.

Both women are complaining now, Bessie about the degradation of the local climate, denouncing it as a symptom of the whole planet being out of whack, while Madame Fenerolo rages against how much time is being wasted on the drive—she hesitates: turn around and catch the A6? Keep on going to Rungis, Belle-Épine, Thiais, and who knows where else, at this rate?

Near Thiais, she turns off the radio, venting some frustration in the process, glad for some quiet . . . A brief respite. The complete halts are growing longer, more frequent; the driver's fingers start drumming on the steering wheel, her shoe is tapping the mat, her eyes dart about jerkily, seeking escape via the rearview mirror or alternatively one of the side windows, even trying to pierce the opacity of the roof before admitting defeat and returning to their initial fixed position, to the great disappointment of the rest of her body.

"Worse than ever!" sighs the driver.

And Bessie seated next to her: "Usually, by this time . . ." A pause before continuing—"traffic's moving," or, "you'd have already dropped me off." And again, she waits a beat before coming back with: "But tonight, well, this is something else . . . !"

On the dashboard clock, the blinking of the little orthogonal sticks means that time's numbers are parading by much faster than those on the odometer. A display of a similar type shows that the outdoor temperature is 33°F, while the inside reading is above 72°. To Bessie, who has kept her coat on over her cardigan, Madame Fenerolo says it would have been wiser to take it off, that staying bundled up like that for too long is the surest way to catch a cold. She doesn't say *take off*, however, but *remove*, and not *coat*, but *wrap*. "Your wrap, Bessie; you should have removed it." And without another word, combining a rotation of her head and a raising of her eyebrows, she indicates the back seat, where, from the beginning of their journey, her own pelisse has lain carefully draped.

11

And likewise from then on, for the sake of ease or precision, or because, in the present circumstances anyway, a gesture is more comforting than words, Bessie, given the choice, resorts to the former rather than the latter.

"And what about Ti-Jus?" Madame Fenerolo asks her.

Bessie stares at the glove compartment, shaking her head in silence before repeating "Ti-Jus," half exclaiming, half questioning in turn, leaving the whole matter hanging in mid-air. Then her hand opens, rises, and falls back flat on her thigh, where it sits inert. Her voice finally adds: "It's hard for young people today," and Madame Fenerolo agrees: with all the problems we're having here at home—she says exactly that, "here at home . . ." These are hardly well-considered choices of words, just some of the usual pat phrases that cross the mind and then slip out whenever they become germane to a conversation in progress. They could easily have been replaced by other such phrases, these commonplaces. And been identical to each other. Even been inverted. Bessie could have said: "With all the problems there are today!" and Madame Fenerolo: "Yes, it's not easy for young people . . ." Their voices, however, the looks on their faces, their faces themselves, the most minute details of their faces—anything about a person that is perceptible from the outside—would nevertheless have registered a significant difference between the two spoken statements: that one meant exactly what its words said, literally, sufficient unto itself; while the other contained a shade of anxious intimacy—where was Ti-Jus? what was he doing? what was to become of him?—and bore the traces of many tender pet names, one after the other, like "Ti-Jus, my baby!" Or, "My boy, my son, my beautiful boy, my Ti-Jus!"

1. 03

As a sideline to her official occupation as a SUMABA cashier, Bessie moonlighted as seamstress at home, in Ris-Orangis, Stairwell H, Mermoz Housing Project. She would sometimes accept an assignment from a colleague, other times from a next-door neighbor; but her steadiest clientele were from the other side of Avenue de Paris, among the female population of the Vallon Apartments, where Madame Fenerolo lived.

Whether she wanted a tailor-made dress or had some trousers that needed altering, a jacket that had to be shortened, it wasn't unusual for the manager to avail herself of the cashier's tax-free talents. Today, it was her skirt, the lining was showing below the hem—had come unstitched, was poorly tailored, or whatever. Did Bessie see . . . ?

This moment was one of those when, suddenly, our guts wrench and our throats constrict—as though these organs have somehow recognized, instinctively, before we ourselves have become fully aware of it, that a crucial change has just taken place: that an era has just ended for all of humanity, or indeed that our own lives have now utterly collapsed. We were walking, or perhaps riding—in a car, on a bike—the entire territory surrounding us was, we felt, an immediate and familiar presence. But then, the road curved, reached a crest; or maybe we did no more than take a single step, and instantly we found ourselves in alien territory: we'd ventured into the beyond, to a land devoid of lagoons or littorals, lacking laterite termite mounds or sandy streets, devoid of coconut palms.

"Look . . ."

Having opened wide and hiked up one of the flaps of her wraparound skirt in order to expose its faulty lining, the manager had also uncovered the upper part of her panty hose, whose transparent quality divulged her glamorous midnight-blue panties as well as the lusterless pallor of her skin. However functional and spontaneous it may have been, this exhibition ought to have been a little embarrassing, disturbing, or, if nothing else, should have established that climate of elementary complicity that binds all individuals of the same sex together within the same generic movements and attitudes as they share in some joint activity. This was not the case here. Nothing equivocal in Madame Fenerolo's gesture. Nothing coquettish. Nor was there any of the friendly and placid abandon of a client consulting with her seamstress. No, there was only a manager's gesture—exclusively and totally that, and thus the dazzlingly obvious fact that for Madame Fenerolo, there existed no possible mode of being aside from that of SUMABA manager. To the extent that, even though the scene progressed uninterrupted—Bessie asking, as she examined the lining, whether the skirt was new or had already been dry-cleaned—it was clear that a brutal event had taken place just the same: one whose troubling effects were already being felt. In the first place, inside the Opel, where the comfort Bessie had formerly felt in the car was now spoiled, ruined, and the ambient air heavy, as before a storm. And then outside, where raging hail had suddenly replaced the rain. And, not satisfied that the future had thus been placed under the indefinite but formidable threat of the present, the past too was now cast in a new light, reactivated in this new context, whereby some particular swing of the wrist, some old widening of the eyes were forcibly reviewed, and "Happy to be living in Ris, aren't you?" or "What's happening with Ti-Jus?" newly reheard. Madame Fenerolo was once again pointing her keychain with its remote control toward the SUMABA. Or she was pointing at the apartment building. Or she was turning off the car radio. Once more she was saying, "I'm going by way of Fontenay" or "I like your new cardigan." Amounting to so many words and actions that, a moment ago, perhaps concealing their true purpose, had seemed innocuous, but which henceforth, crudely, would go on to reveal that all things were subjugated to the sole principle of manager-being: the car radio and the streetlights, the security guards at the SUMABA or the Île-de-France residents—those *Franciliens*, stuck in bumper-to-bumper traffic—Bessie's cardigan, Bessie herself, or even Ti-Jus, her beautiful son. And summoned in this way to be subsumed within this principle, seeking by nature to negate their individual existences on pain of being deemed utterly meaningless, all the aforementioned entities, confined in the hermetically sealed cabin of the metallic gray Opel, vibrated silently with the same spirit of refusal, and under the thunderous hammering of hail maintained the highly charged, stifling atmosphere, suffused with violence—as sometimes happens when, in the face of the unacceptable, one's sense of humiliation wells up from deep inside oneself, quivering for a long tense moment before erupting in a cry of rage, or even an act of brute force.

1. 04

The long RER has just left from Track 2, laying bare, under the neon lights, the double rail of steel, the okoume ties, and the ballast strewn with wastepaper stinking of urine. On the other side of Platform A, the seven twenty-one bound for Corbeil-Essones via Ris-Orangis waits its turn, not as packed as the previous local trains, but full enough that most of the benches and jump seats are taken. The passengers are dozing, looking out the window or reading, chatting in twos, in groups. Nearly everyone displays the serenity of people who feel sheltered from the unexpected, secure in belonging to an imminent future that will unfold without their having to move a muscle. Thus, the moment will come when the loud-speakers will make their final announcement. The doors will slide shut automatically, slamming in unison. It will be time. The train will start off. It will gradually surface from underground, finally emerge abruptly into the open air, and then trundle on through the vast night, following the immutable course of the Paris-Corbeil line via Ris-Orangis, with its like-wise immutable sequence of stops, each one thinning out the passenger load in turn.

Then, just before the stroke of twenty-one minutes after the hour, voices resound, both distorted and amplified by the faraway corridors of Level -1: youthful voices whose whoops and shouts punctuate their already lively forward motion. Inside the Paris-Corbeil train, the mood shifts from passive expectation to a mixture of surprise, anxiety, and curiosity. Legs cross and uncross, feet slip underneath seats, buttocks squirm in search of a sweeter spot. The youthful voices, meanwhile, have advanced so quickly that they're now resounding in the cavernous, unobstructed space of the gallery upstairs, coupled with noises that—as they filter down to the -2 level, where the trains are boarded—give rise to images of the following acts in the minds of the waiting passengers: crushing a soda can in the palm of one's hand, tossing it into the air, kicking it, soccer-style; on the way, applying a karate chop to the side of a ticket dispenser or punching through the sound-proofing of a phone booth. The spinal columns in the Paris-Corbeil have all straightened, torsos have all spun round. More anxious with each passing second, all eyes are on the stairs that lead from the upstairs gallery to the platform. The approaching youths are undoubtedly drunk. Perhaps completely out of their minds. And even though the shouts sometimes melt into bursts of laughter, it takes no small effort for the passengers, hearing these sounds from afar, to force themselves to believe that the authors of this mayhem are only having fun, and not murdering one another—so raucous is the pandemonium that will be tumbling onto Platform A, any second now, to take the seven twenty-one train by storm.

Indifferent to these goings-on, the loudspeakers announce the departure. They designate the train by its number and give the names of the stations where stops will be made. They enumerate "Maisons-Alfort, Villeneuve, Juvisy, Viry, Grigny, Ris-Orangis . . ."

Then, at the foot of the stairs, four boys in their late teens emerge and make a run for it, shouting, only to disperse and then converge onto the last car. One of them, coming to a halt, blocks open the sliding doors that are about to close. Another does the same with the next set down. Yet another boy trips, or pretends to trip, and finishes the race at a hop, or else exaggerating the momentum that propels him into the car, grabbing the vertical bar meant for standing passengers and twirling around it three times before coming to a stop. Then, as the train starts moving and gradually picks up speed, in a few strides too disproportionately flamboyant for the tight space of the central aisle, two of the boys walk back to join their companions, so that here they are, all four, out of breath, laughing it up, shaking their heads, and repeating endlessly the same exclamations punctuated by the same swearword, as is common among accomplices when evoking some recent, shared, reckless escapade.

At present, the other passengers are taking up less room in the compartment. They are also less individualized, bound together now by the fearful hostility they feel toward these unruly youths they're being forced to ride with, having no idea what lunatic notion might now come into their heads, what new stunt they might improvise, whether their next move will be swift, precise, and brutal, or slow, expansive, and awkward . . . The newly arrived foursome are in constant conversation. They exchange beginnings of phrases more often than complete sentences, to which they add various interjections and sound effects. At times, the whole car resounds with some rude remark, with several simultaneous retorts, or else some less-articulated outcry prompted by nothing and addressed to no one in particular . . . Without even having to think, the silent witnesses to this vocalizing identify the language they are hearing as French. Nevertheless, certain formulations sound odd to their ears; they can't quite make out certain words, or when they can, these seem to make no sense—as in the word *Nucifera* that one of the youths utters in annoyance when he tries unsuccessfully to open a door while the train is moving.

"What's with this Nucifera!"

"Spadices, dude, spadices!" says another, mockingly, both emphasizing and elongating the *a*.

A third has gone over to rattle the handle on the bathroom door. He begs emphatically: "It's an emergency!" Pleased with his little joke, with his three friends looking on, he alludes to the *coir* of a *drupe*—says *drupe coir*, in fact, in the same sentence where he's just slurred *I can see from here* into *Ikn see from here*.

18

Because they use words like these—much more than because they're brawny, restless, and voluble—the four adolescents in the Paris-Corbeil look like alien creatures: as foreign as winged angels, as subtropical sprites, or as young and dangerous pagan gods whose slightest prank would surely have unleashed a catastrophe upon mere mortals. And as for the uninitiated, since they know nothing of the jargon they're hearing, they focus their attention on intonation and body language. Depending on whether the boys' legs are in motion or torsos are swaying in the train's vibrations, whether their breathing is accelerated or a steady rhythm is being maintained in their speech; whether lips and teeth along with tongues and palates have hardened or loosened the pronunciation of consonants, the passengers sense that, for the moment, the foursome's mood is either bellicose or peaceful, and thus that the immediate future is either auspicious or ill-fated for their compartment. But deprived as they are of the crutch of language, reduced to apprehending nothing but physical signals and assigning them meaning based solely on intuition, the passengers of the Paris-Corbeil have been demoted to an animal state, excluded from *Homo loquens*; or, worse, have found themselves compelled upon reflection to admit that, when it really comes down to it, the "Talking Animal" itself may be, essentially, at a loss for words.

Thus, as much to escape such introspection as to flee the outward threat, many a gaze is turning toward the steamed-up windows that serve to isolate them from the cold outside and seal them off from the sedentary world. These gazes cling to the polychrome reflections that blend into the uniformly gray, vaguely incandescent cloudscape—the effect of urban lighting on the night—mitigating, via their own consistency, the inconsistency of the images streaming past. Views flash by in quick succession, each as brief and taut as the next. Then, a moment of total darkness before the fitful stream resumes, the embankment with its clumps of grass and cracked concrete, the Corbeil-Paris-Gare de Lyon train coming from the other direction, passing in a cyclonic din, then the embankment again, a graffitied wall, a switching tower, and other bits of landscape so nearby that they pass more relentlessly than the retina can accommodate, with only intermittent rests, when the flatness of a vacant lot or some rail junction broadens the field of vision and pushes the scattered silhouettes of electrical pylons, Lombardy poplars, and apartment towers to the horizon.

The four youths, meanwhile, haven't stopped their fidgeting and chatter. One, despite the pictograms that prohibit smoking, has lit a cigarette. Another combs his hair, feet spread apart, knees bent, back arched in order to better frame the blurry image reflected back by the imperfect mirror of the night. And still another, whose ears have disappeared beneath the headphones of his Walkman, is beating out the rhythm with his shoulders, lifting and dropping them in turn, extending and retracting his neck, sneakers lightly marking time on the anti-skid surface. The last of them lifts a finger vehemently skyward.

"That's what I call bumping the stipe, man!"

The boy next to him goes him one better. From *machete* he makes the verb *machetty*; from *conflagration, conflagro*. He says that, back at Thingy, at Whatsit, at Whatcha-callit, if they keep making *conflagro* with the *copra*, one of these days, he's going to *machetty* their *aerial roots*.

A few steps away, forever coifing himself into his composite reflection, the boy with the comb co-opts *machetty* and *aerial roots*. Smiling broadly, he repeats "machetty their aerial roots" several times until, words and features in sync, he shifts expressions and hangs back with his friend, the one grooving to his Walkman, thumb pointing to the other half of their party.

"Hey, what about those guys? They seen your new switchblade?"

In fact, this is a translation: he uses slang instead of "seen" and "new"—just as he says "switch" and not "switchblade." And without waiting for the answer to his question:

"Hey, you two!" he calls. "Scope the switch on Ti-Jus!"

1. 05

Perhaps it was his halo of wooly hair, his aerial silhouette, and a certain solar luster emanating from his person that all made Ti-Jus so popular with the girls. Willingly, women or young girls would allow themselves to come into contact with his skin, pressing their dresses or jeans, their undergarments, their bare flesh to it fearlessly; and were one to approach him from a distance, she would scarcely have glimpsed the young man before she'd get excited, and, using the excuse of a girlfriend lagging behind, would turn around—"We're almost there!"—and by this ruse defer, for a suave, coquettish moment, the declaration that her euphoric face was burning to make to Ti-Jus.

And yet, he hungered for more. He would have liked to be the object of even more adulation, even greater devotion; to have countless lovers, and in locations vastly more accommodating than the cement basements of the Mermoz Housing Project. Thus it was that—just as dreams encroach so shamelessly on our interior spaces, encouraged by sleep but adapting to the waking state as well—thoughts of "girl" inhabited Ti-Jus night and day, sometimes subsuming his consciousness entirely, other times taking possession of only those idle parts of his organism and mobilizing them for action, unbeknownst to his conscious mind, attending to some other business.

This was borne out on the Paris-Corbeil.

The mute gymnastics of his lips, the intermittent snapping of fingers, the rhythmic swaying of his silhouette accompanying the ground bass vibrations leaking from his headphones—this combination of movements testified that Ti-Jus, for the most part, if not entirely, had his mind on music. What little attention remained, he granted to his friends—though sparingly now, using a play of facial expressions and gestures rather than words to keep up his end of their dialogue, and without allowing direct eye contact to become a part of either. As a result, the young man's eyes were free to roam. They might have lingered on the windows, mused at the odd assortment of real and reflected objects displayed there, or remained nonchalantly at rest in the quivering, striated half-light of their lashes. And yet, they kept busy. Methodically, and with even more resolve than if his mind were actually at work, they scanned the seated passengers. They drew a continuous horizontal line across the faces, halting suddenly, zipping into reverse, stopping once again, and, after a blink or two of their lids, commencing a kind of expert appraisal. They gauged someone's height, estimated someone's size, assessed a particular area of their bodies, appraised its volume, circumference, degree of ripeness . . . And nothing impeded his eyes from conducting their business entirely independent of any other ongoing bodily process—neither the rhythmic jolting of his shoulders, nor the pinching of his lips, accompanying some new soaring melisma, nor what was to follow: fingers lifting his headphones to momentarily liberate his ears, the hand that went searching for the switchblade deep in his inside pocket, the wrist action coordinated with the thumb, releasing the spring-loaded blade . . . The steel gleamed—dense, hard, sharp. His friends moved in and leaned forward, in perfect synchrony, above the knife. Their faces beaming with childlike admiration, they outdid each other in their awe and exclamations, dragging out the vowels of a *yeah*, delineating the four syllables of *son of a bitch*, or, in a more technical and slangy mode, making reference to a *trunk of twenty-five*, a *bouquet of fourteen*, or *aerial roots*.

Meanwhile, the pressure exerted on the backs and lumbar plexuses of the seated passengers had begun to subside, matched by an appreciable modification in the equilibrium of those standing. Outside, the elements of landscape grew rarer and more stable. One could better identify them, better tally them. Soon these elements would comprise a single fixed image, void of any life apart from the tentative footfalls and steamy breath of the handful of remaining passengers overjoyed that the train had finally arrived at the Maisons-Alfort station.

Two girls boarded the last car, immediately piquing the boys' interest. Moving with that particular variety of slowness that's really nothing more than suppressed haste, and often a prelude to an attack, Ti-Jus pocketed his "switch" and, after cutting off the sound on his Walkman, let the flexible arc of its headset slip down around his neck. His three companions were strutting, awkward in their attempts at poise, though efficient enough in deploying an encirclement maneuver. Their eyes forever on the prowl, their comments to one another—supposedly addressing the company at large—were only efforts to attract the attention of the new arrivals. Then, the girls were addressed more straightforwardly. So, where were they coming from? Where were they headed? What were their names . . . ? Hadn't the four boys already met them somewhere—on this same Paris-Corbeil train, or at some mutual friend's, or at the Coco Bar in Juvisy, or at the Évry Bowling Alley . . . ? The girls made no reply. Facing each other, they merely shrugged and breathed sighs of boredom. But as the boys' encirclement maneuver reached completion, their questions being posed from nearer and nearer to the girls' bodies, the latter suddenly switched tactics.

The first to turn and face the boys—the less frail of the twosome under threat from the four-pronged formation leaning ever closer—asked in an unwavering voice whether the guys hadn't already had enough of a gust on their fronds. "Because of the trade winds," she added, seeming to suggest that this was hardly the proper time, season, or latitude. And in conclusion:

23

"So, listen up! . . . Back into your hole, *gusbirs!*"

The boys, though they'd hardly beat a retreat over so little, did nonetheless mark a pause in their procedure. They feigned astonishment, laying on the irony for laughs—"A spadix like her! . . . A bract like that! . . ."—while tempering their arrogance, allowing themselves to admit a certain amount of esteem for this girl who spoke the same slang as theirs. With that, the tension between the masculine quartet and the girlish duo would almost certainly have diminished—and, proportionately, the unease felt by the other passengers—had it not been for the violent intervention of the second girl from Maisons-Alfort . . . the smaller of the two *Maisonnaises*. Sheltered to this point in her friend's shadow, silently at work rubbing her chin with the distended neck of her sky-blue sweater, she suddenly lashed out: her head thrust forward, arms stretched out behind her, and eyes apoplectic, she started out addressing the boys with insults derived from the common repertory, before getting into the coconut-palm slang:

"I *hispine* you!" she raved. "I *hispine* you, get it . . . ?"

And shouting louder still:

"I'm gonna be weaving your coir!"

Screaming now, more high-pitched:

"I've got your *stipe dugout!*"

And finally, as if in a daze, her voice husky, growing more hoarse: you *spathes*, you *saps* . . . she had them *oozing*, she made them *ferment*; and with that, she freaked the fuck out of them.

As for the boys: while two of his sidekicks mumbled inaudible retorts inspired by the same insults they'd just been subjected to, Ti-Jus, unaccompanied by music this time, resumed the dance number he had been doing to his Walkman. Only the hulk with the comb was smiling broadly, innocently—too thick, it would seem, to feel affronted by the girl's curses, or even to diagnose a fit of hysterics.

Nor, indeed, did he seem aware of having jostled anyone when, pushing forward almost involuntarily, he shoved the first girl aside in order to slip behind the second one. In a flash, the girl in the blue sweater was immobilized, elbows behind her back and heels off the ground . . . Squirming and kicking, jerking and biting, she tried to wriggle free any way she could, but only managed to get red in the face and mess up her hair. From above, the boy with the comb was grinning all the wider now.

"Who wants a piece?" he offered.

His friends responded with excited if still tentative facial expressions—an unclenching of teeth, a general relaxation of features, while nostrils remained slightly flared, or tongues continued to roll beneath skin, moving a bump around an inner cheek in slow motion.

All around, some of the passengers wagged their heads, a sickly smile on their faces—which was their way of maintaining that all this commotion wasn't really amounting to anything nasty. Others, as though barely restraining themselves from intervening, gave a slight wiggle of heroic indignation; while still others acted as though they hadn't seen a thing, despite the mounting evidence that something disastrous was about to happen right under their noses. Because, despite multiple attempts by the as-yet-unmolested girl to intercede—"Come on, quit screwing around!," "Cut the crap!," or "Is this what you guys are like?"—the male excitement was growing. Worse, it was changing form. The four late adolescents, who together had foisted their physicality onto the scene in the train-car right from the start, and whose subsequent movements, however varied they may have been from one boy to the next, had nonetheless composed a well-regulated choreography—these same four were now getting increasingly agitated, and each in his own way. One stamped, as if pawing the ground, marking time, a fleeting wave running up his body to the back of his neck with each tread, bending him first in one direction, then the other. His neighbor stuck out his chest, broadening his shoulders; while a third, to keep a lock of hair out of his face, repeated the same cervical twist, over and over again, accompanied each time by a fresh snort, his head thus tossed around at the end of the neck as though swept up by some powerful cyclone. As for the boy with the comb, he was all-enveloping. Thorax concave, shoulders collapsed forward, his hand ventured doggedly toward a certain fastener, a certain zipper, a certain clasp, or some other piece of wardrobe-hardware holding his prisoner together. And making the commotion caused by their struggling bodies all the more intense, the voices issuing from the melee did so at such a rate as to prevent the sounds from forming into real words as they poured through their mouths; so that, with the exception of several *weave the leaves*, some hate-filled *in palisade formation*s, some panic-stricken *make some for yourself*s, some *mats*, some *fans*, and some *sliding shutters*, all belched out by the girl in the blue sweater, the last car of the Paris-Corbeil resounded with something less like human voices than some primal wind—muted, cavernous, and rising without warning to a strident pitch, like some random eolian howl.

But at the word *palisade*—since it had come to the Lyon Bridge and was now running above the water—the train had begun to slow down. By *eolian*, in fact, it had come to a stop, at the same time that the lights went off throughout the entire train. An extended silence fell in the last car, during which a wave of outdoor air surged through the compartment, bringing the sweetish smell of river water in with the cold. The hulk with the comb had let go of the girl in the blue sweater. She had stopped screaming. Already calmed down, reconciled as if by magic, and chaste once again in the new darkness that engulfed them, the six adolescents huddled together in front of the exit door to gaze out at the broad, black flow of the Seine. Trees rose up on either bank, stripped of their leaves by the winter but still dense enough to form a mass so opaque in the night as to eliminate any trace of a city from the landscape. No more buildings, high-rises, or houses to be seen from the Lyon Bridge; no more alleys or streets, no more roads or highways; nothing but level water, with vegetation silhouetted at the river's edge and the sky forming a dome above the water and vegetation both. And alone in the world, from this particular angle, or at least buffered from the material *Francilien* reality, just as they were from the other passengers who had presently retreated into the gloom, Ti-Jus, his two new girlfriends, and his three friends all gazed intensely downstream, where, as though from some silent boat, they were watching for the next bend in the river, hopeful that a slow ebb tide would greet them with foam and eddies, and that, on dry land, set back from the shore, the dark, jagged crest of the tapering forest would bristle with the first coconut palms—a sight that, in advance, inspired a great sense of relief, even bliss, in the little group on the lookout, now dazzled twice over: once by the spectacle of a dream fulfilled, and then, by the fact that this dream could exist in their conscious minds at the same time as it was materializing before their eyes.

1. 06

It might also happen that the stretch of water is ocean, with belvedere instead of the Lyon Bridge as the edge of the coconut grove, whence we gaze out to sea. We then try to imagine other shores beyond the horizon; but however well versed we may be in the range and dispersion of earthly locales, we can envision only a few. And among these, several exist for us in name only; or they are nothing more than shapes, a monochrome spot on a piece of paper, a tiny square, a dot, and in the end, only attaining some semblance of binding reality if we've actually visited them, once upon a time, or have heard them spoken of over the course of years in private conversations.

Likewise, as new stars would do against the primeval chaos, the SUMABA in Bagneux stood out of the coal-black and russet Île-de-France night, as did the Vallon Apartments and the Mermoz Housing Project in Ris-Orangis, the TWC building, Orly Airport, the town of Juvisy with the station where the Paris-Corbeil is currently arriving, and the avenue where Madame Fenerolo's metallic gray Opel has just turned. On the terraced rooftop of Traffic Watch Central, two radar antennae slowly rotate. Fifteen kilometers away, in front of the SUMABA, a security guard in a tracksuit has stepped into the parking lot, preceded at a distance by a watchdog just let off its leash. At Orly, a plane is about to land, another about to take off. Bessie Deux-Rivières and Madame Fenerolo in the Opel, as well as Tis-Jus and the other passengers on the Paris-Corbeil, can follow the sloping ascent of the second aircraft, whose blinking lights move in concert: disappearing momentarily, reappearing further on, higher up, before plunging definitively into the night. The SUMABA security guard, head scrunched between his shoulders and backbone bent against the cold rain, retraces his steps as if to seek shelter, but stops midway, turns around, and whistles for his dog, then calling: "Bucco! . . . Bucco, Bucco! . . ." The girl in the blue sweater tugs at Ti-Jus by the sleeve while pointing at the new set of blinking lights rising above the high-tension wires. Can the boy tell what kind of plane it is this time? How high it's going to climb? How many passengers are on board, and where it's heading . . . ? In Ris-Orangis, on the fifth floor of the Vallon Apartments, darkness has stolen over the apartment of Madame Fenerolo, while at the Deux-Rivières household, on the other side of the avenue, the ceiling light inside the front door is lit, as are those in the living room, the hanging lamp in the dining area, and the wall lamps on either side of the sofa bed. The kitchen is also lit up. That's where Celestin is standing, busy rinsing off the camping knife he's just used to slice some chorizo. While standing, performing this act of rinsing, as well as later on, in front of the window next to the gas stove, when his nails lightly scrape the glass pane as he parts the curtain that latticed his field of vision, or as he pads back into the living room at a measured pace, Celestin has a peculiar bearing, left shoulder raised, left arm slanted, left fist clenched tight, as though clutching, enraged, at some absent weight . . . The noises Celestin's movements produce, breaking up the silence, are distinct and fleeting in the apartment. The sounds emanating from elsewhere, just like the smells, which at their own pace and via their own routes have likewise converged upon the apartment, are organized into less well-defined ensembles, arriving in succession, or else one atop the other—overlapping or separate, depending on the ear or nose in question, or a whim of the imagination. Thus, an argument in the stairwell and the long, crashing descent of trash going down the garbage chute resound concomitantly. Or else, the reek of cooked fat spreading from floor to floor is accompanied by the continuous drone of television sets and the intermittent voices of neighbors. Or again, rising up from the avenue, the scent of exhaust fumes is momentarily superseded by a burst of winter air, just as it occasionally happens that the distant sound of traffic is drowned out by an ambulance siren, or by music on a boom box turned all the way up, or by the approaching rumble of a helicopter, or by someone's calling out a name . . . To all this, Celestin remains indifferent, equally aloof from his surroundings and the objects located there, despite his unhurried, determined movement from room to room. His features remain impassive. His gaze, beneath heavy lids, comes to rest on nothing in particular: not so much elusive as drawn to a point apparently beyond the boundaries of visible space. And this marks his face with a sense of despondency, a certain resigned passivity that is as incompatible with the tension of his left arm, the fierce flexing of his fist, as it is with the ceremonious restraint displayed by the rest of the body; such that violence, melancholy, and solemnity, three incompatible states, are occurring together, simultaneously and implausibly, in a single man, who has, seemingly, been canceled out by them, gutted: akin, in his temporary solitude, to those ghosts reputed to return to the land of the living every evening at a fixed hour, in order to act out past crimes; or else to those ordinary individuals chosen by fate to commit some unspeakable act, in order to fulfill the destiny of the rest of the species, and who, burning with shame, take pity on themselves at the very moment of their glory.

Then comes the time when the noise from a motor—after breaking away from the mass of sound in which, at first, it had been subsumed, indistinct—can be identified as a car driving down Beuilhet Alley, which leads to the Mermoz Housing Project. The car slows down on its approach, then parks a couple of feet from Stairwell H. Two metallic car doors slam shut, one after the other. This double report rises up to Celestin, joined by the voices of Madame Fenerolo and Bessie saying (the former): "What time does that mean you'll be having dinner?" and then (the second): "Oh, it's no big deal," and then, again (the former): "You sure?" and (the latter): "It's just a fitting, it won't take long," and (the former): "If that's what you want, Bessie," or else "Fine," or else "All right, let's do it, then . . . So when do you think I'll be getting it back?"

Madame Fenerolo has come up to Bessie's on several previous occasions so that Bessie could take her measurements, and she even came a week ago for the same pantsuit that the above *it* was referring to, in the question *when do you think I'll be getting it back*. Yet today, despite these previous visits, the moment she enters the building, she glances around, as though to get her bearings, and then, at each landing, before each flight of stairs, she hesitates briefly.

The two women are out of breath by the time they get up to Bessie's place. Madame Fenerolo says, "These apartments are actually . . ."—except that she didn't say *apartments*: "These *units* are actually . . ." Then, at a distance, to Celestin, "Oh, hello Celestin." And later: "That's so dated," "Not that simple, not by a long shot," "That's just people talking," or "No they don't, come on, what makes you say a thing like that . . . ?" She's removed her pelisse while talking, and after a quick scan of the room, has laid it on the back of the sofa bed. She's glanced out the window, through the white sheer curtains. She's also looked at the photograph of Ti-Jus as a child, in a glass frame set in full view atop the television. She's picked up the framed picture to have a closer look, and putting it back down, has taken care to place it exactly where it was, at the same angle—while moving the ashtray slightly away from the frame, then adjusting the houseplant next to the ashtray by a few degrees . . . A loud noise is heard from the kitchen where Celestin has retreated. Her actions suspended in mid-motion, head immobile but eyes turned laterally as far as possible toward the source of the noise, Bessie inquires from afar: "Are you all right?"

No answer.

Moving quickly, she arrives at the threshold of the kitchen, and from there observes—or has addressed to her—some indication that it's nothing serious: something dropped, a fall, a rebound off the tile floor, shards in the sink. Madame Fenerolo, about to join Bessie, inquires what's happened. She says "So?" and raises her eyebrows and stretches her neck—to which Bessie replies, "It's alright, nothing serious." Then, having commenced their return to the living-room area in unison, their visual awareness lagging behind their automatic motor functions, the two women suddenly tremble, almost jump back in surprise, finding that Ti-Jus is standing there in front of them.

1.07

To his mother's "You're home . . . ? We didn't hear you come in!" the son replies with a mumble in which there persists an indistinct residue of something like *yes* or *yeah* and *mom*. In counterpoint, his hand executes a gesture that—were his fingers and palm straightened into a more rigid, martial flatness, instead of remaining loose, forming a hollow, looking as though they were ready to catch a basketball, or else to caress, delicately, the curve of the mother's cheek—could have passed for an injunction to halt. Their exchange is reduced to this virtual caress, to that mumbled response. Ti-Jus does not greet the manager. He has seen her, to be sure, but still fails to greet her, or even to acknowledge her presence. Does such conspicuous apathy spring from long-standing acquaintance, or from what Ti-Jus has just seen and heard—that is, the manager-voice uttering an interrogative "so," the manager-spine and the manager-neck stretched toward the kitchen, both elbows bent, pointed backward, the manager-chest nearing Bessie's shoulder . . . ? Whatever the case, the adolescent, as though prompted by disgust or some fixation, has turned away from the two women, still surprised at his stealthy arrival. Without further ado, he goes to his room, which he then promptly exits, heading for the kitchen, soon leaving the kitchen for the bathroom, each of these departures requiring that he pass through the living-room: the double impact of his shoes resounding on the floor, a muffled and succinct verbal exchange, extended hydraulic noises . . . When he once again crosses the living-room, Bessie lets him know that she'll be needing a moment alone with her client. She says that Madame Fenerolo has come for a fitting—says exactly that: "Madame Fenerolo has come for a fitting." Ti-Jus pretends not to hear. He avoids his mother's gaze, whistles under his breath, takes his time, obviously driven by a stubborn desire to be contrary. Because, apart from his silent refusal of the request just made of him, and not content that his very presence is wholly in defiance of the visitor's, each of his actions, and even the attitude of his posture, seem to call into question the theater of their performance, there in the apartment, to the extent that—observing him in the flesh—one could even think that Ti-Jus were actually somewhere else, busying himself with something altogether different from everyday bathroom ablutions or the simple exigencies entailed by one's return to the domestic turf after a day spent with his friends. Thus, coming out of the bathroom, barefoot, naked from the waist up, a towel tossed over his shoulder and boom box in hand, it looks for a moment as though the Deux-Rivières boy will head to his room—but no, he's stopped. And turned now toward the living-room, he scans the area panoramically, seeming to enlarge the space before him, seeking out some silhouette in the far distance, or else just a place to sit down, alone, right on the floor. He then starts pacing, slowly, looking at the floor all around him as though keeping an eye out for the furtive and repeated appearances of some little burrowing creatures. As he does so, he uses his foot—with the agility of a soccer player—to pick up a ball of yarn that's rolled onto the parquet-finished concrete. Pausing then, he leans back casually against the wallpaper, against a doorframe. He blinks. He turns his head. With the towel, he wipes the inside of an ear or pats his hair dry . . . Walls, partitions, and the furniture placed around the room all have an equal lack of bearing on the actions and movements of Ti-Jus; rather, these obstructions organize, or reorganize, the stage set on which Ti-Jus blocks out his moves—as though the laws of matter have been replaced by those of some all-powerful authority, capable of arranging or removing the obstacles in a living-room at will, and capable as well of generating tropical heat and coconut colors, even though it's winter, and nighttime, and even though Ris-Orangis, at 48° 38' northern latitude, is located well outside the Nucifera biome.

By way of apology, Bessie flashes a weary smile at the manager, who replies in the same silent code—an air, a gesture, implying "Never mind," "That's how they are at that age," and "Hey, I'm no prude" all at once. Indeed, Madame Fenerolo shows no sign that she's been in any way offended, nor that she's experiencing the least discomfort at the hostility and persistence of Ti-Jus. While removing her high heels, even starting to unhook her wraparound skirt, she asks whether she should also take off her turtleneck sweater . . . She's raised her voice, Bessie having left her momentarily to go get the pantsuit from the front hall closet. Now dressed in only her pantyhose and her turtleneck, the manager asks again, still acting oblivious, if she can have the lining mended, whether it'll be all right to leave her wraparound skirt with Bessie tomorrow.

"I'll bring it with me to the SUMABA," she says.

Adding that there's no hurry, though.

1. 08

Between the epigastrium and the pelvic region, in among the meanderings of our entrails, there germinates Refusal. We don't feel its corpuscular presence at first: only a thermal shift, an icy cold welling up from a place deep within us—deep, but nonetheless as far from the self as possible—and which, spreading unobstructed into our bodies, assumes the form of a thousand filaments merging with the complex network of our nerves. This intermingling disrupts the entire organism, all the way to the epidermal level, where, reacting to a phenomenon normally restricted to the viscera, the skin pales here, flushes there, and everywhere starts to crawl. Finally, when it outgrows the belly—as do pain or rage in similar circumstances—Refusal is externalized. It consolidates. It grows denser. It tapers off and shoots into the air to deploy its powerful waves of energy into the upper reaches of the enclosing space. And in doing so, it designs this space anew, reestablishing the curves and verticality that allow us to comprehend gentleness and stand upright, the vanishing point that allows us to come and go freely, and the shadows that afford us a leisurely contemplation of full sunlight, and by making use of the same surroundings that have always shaped our lives, it reinvents the landscape as one capable of allaying our fears.

Yet, in the Deux-Rivières home, had such germination not taken place—had the unmistakable swell of Refusal not risen up in the living room, been deployed beneath the yellowed plasterboard ceiling—Madame Fenerolo would have occupied the entire field. Long after her departure, the idea of her, of the manager-being, would have continued, triumphantly, to haunt the apartment, arousing, as an indirect result—omnipresent, and itself as though suspended in the atmosphere—a bitter, shameful sense of submission.

This particular worst-case scenario was avoided.

Still, hardly has the body emerged unscathed from this kind of close call than it betrays how heavily the future weighs upon its spirit. With each passing day, the shoulders cave a bit more. The eyes avoid contact with other eyes, out of fear; they glaze over from exhaustion. Henceforth more downhearted than violent, than solemn, Celestin—when he isn't going round in his endless circles—stays flopped down on the sofa bed, staring at the same virtual point in space, fiddling with his own hands, his camping knife, the can of alcohol-free beer or the glass of water he's just finished. Even Ti-Jus is subdued. As for Bessie, she still feels compelled to speak every so often, to feel sorry for the neighbor who's down with a cold, to remark on the overnight frost, anything, just so long as a voice is still heard in the apartment, at least intermittently. But mostly, she keeps quiet. Or else, on the verge of saying something—to her son: "We're out of bread, you'll have to pick some up"; to her husband: "Turn on the TV, have some fun!" or "Why don't you go out for a walk?"—she'll suddenly decide against it, as though lacking the strength to pronounce so many words.

Should a door slam, in this obsidian-dark setting, should a water pipe suddenly shudder or a windowpane vibrate because of a low-flying jet, the unexpected noise is immediately translated into the sound of some terrible death agony—at once a desperate plea for survival and an outraged protest against the inanity of fate. The rest of the time, dismay prevails. And how can one not succumb to it, in the long run? What possibility of retort? What hope of flight? Why not capitulate here and now . . . ? A pre-snowfall light pervades each day without fail, drab and yet so permeating, so universal and unvarying, that no electric light can manage to accurately demarcate any of the buildings outside, nor even to define any interior space; and since the weather reports are forecasting no change, it seems inevitable that the third floor left-hand Stairwell H at the Mermoz Housing Project will have to give way, sooner or later, and merge, amid the grayness, with all the other Ris-Orangis locations and lodgings, just as Ris-Orangis itself will soon become one with all localities of Île-de France. Of course, neither the number of *départements* nor their boundary lines will change. Among the one-thousand-odd urban districts that make up the region, some diversity will endure. The rivers Oise and Marne, the Seine and the Orge or the Yvette will still contrast with terra firma, as will hills with valleys, plains with plateaus, metropolitan areas with undeveloped zones. Yet, the river waters will look stagnant, as paralyzed as the trees made leafless by winter. Here and there, in the dismal landscape, long, rectangular housing blocks will resemble recumbent towers. And the highways raised upon concrete piers will give the impression that the ground has collapsed all around them, or that a cataclysm has laid waste to everything, flattened whatever was once standing, except perhaps the highway construction works, a drab panorama of pylons overlooking the automobile graveyards and trailer parks, while a water tower or a steeple silhouetted against the horizon will stand out as the solitary survivors peering over the precipice at the end of the world.

Eleven, twelve days go by under these conditions—one and a half of which go by without the SUMABA—the time it takes for Bessie to mend the lining of the wraparound skirt and to finish the pantsuit and pack them both up before going to drop them off.

Ti-Jus offers his services.

"Do you want me to go?"

Or he says it some other way.

"Leave it," he says, "I'll take care of it."

He takes a shower. He shampoos, rinses, lathers up, and rinses again, taking his time. Linked to the thought of how cold it is outside, the scalding water awakens a longing in him for summertime, with its cool rains, just as the cramped stall and the steam fogging up the bathroom make him long for wide-open spaces, fresh air, and a downpour in the rainy season, streaming down his vertical body, delayed in its descent only by its passage through the tightly-woven filter of his hair before reaching the scalp.

He shaves. In the mirror above the sink, in order to ease the spreading of the lather and then the scraping of the blade along his jawline, Ti-Jus's features remain expressionless, thereby imparting a certain gravitas to his movements, like a solemn acquiescence to the course of action that the grooming of his face has already begun to fulfill.

Back in his room, he chooses the clothes he will wear. He selects the best he has: his newest socks, his favorite pair of underpants, the T-shirt printed with his own portrait, and his motorcycle jacket: red, with blue shoulder guards and cuffs . . . While he dresses, the sounds produced by Celestin, opening the refrigerator door or coughing repeatedly, come through the partition wall. Shortly afterwards, there's the muffled voice of Bessie, who's discovered the sopping bathroom, and Ti-Jus's towel rolled up into a ball, and the sink left unrinsed. She says "Again!" regarding the splashed water and the bunched-up towel; "Just like his father," glancing at the unrinsed sink. Weary and half resigned, half angry, she's on the verge of adding something like "It's always me who has to . . ." or "It's really not that hard to . . ." when the sudden ringing of the doorbell interrupts her.

The visitor is the same friend of Ti-Jus's who, on the Paris-Corbeil train, had lifted the girl in the blue sweater off the ground; likewise the same friend who'd jiggled the handle to the train's bathroom, and who'd combed his hair gazing into the lateral window, and who'd been so entranced by the idea, or rather the statement, about "machettying aerial roots." Bessie knows him. And so, anticipating the question the boy is about to ask, she indicates, with a tilt of her head, a vague direction in the apartment, adding, without specifying who she means:

"He's in there . . ." Pronouncing the *zin*, eliding the *he*.

At the moment when his friend enters his bedroom, Ti-Jus, one knee on the ground, is finishing lacing up his sneakers. He has donned his chicest pair of jeans, which are also the heaviest and most tidily slit: a slash below the left knee, a gash to the right of the groin. Now he need only pull on his bright yellow heavy wool sweater over the T-shirt, and then his leather motorcycle jacket over the bright yellow sweater, and he'll be ready. But without waiting until the procedure is complete, his friend opens his mouth, leaving it gaping for a moment, finally letting out a "Nucif!," a "Cifera!," or some other laudatory exclamation; or if he emits nothing but a squeak, it's still a sufficiently expressive one to signify that, absolutely, an outfit like that one will dazzle the girls.

1. 09

Out of either temperamental reserve or a special contemplative state unique to this day, and in either case unnervingly ungracious, Ti-Jus says nothing, carries on uninterrupted, fails to even turn around to note his friend's arrival. He stands back up, appreciating from above the double-bowed knot he's just tied on his sneaker. Then he does a couple of deep knee bends to soften up his jeans, so that knees and hips as well as penis and testicles assume their proper places. The friend ventures some slangy wordplay—*indecent* for *indehiscent*, and something about his *drupe* drooping. But Ti-Jus goes about his business in solemn silence. He pulls on his bright yellow sweater. He sprinkles a little aftershave onto the sleeves. He empties out the pockets of the cotton jacket worn the previous day, transferring their contents to those of his leather jacket . . . his ID card in its plastic sleeve, some small change, and his switchblade pass from one article of clothing to the next, still without Ti-Jus making the slightest acknowledgement of his friend's presence.

And yet, far from being offended by the chilly welcome, the friend stays upbeat, keeps things playful, and coaxes Ti-Jus to get into the same mood.

"Hey, scope this!" he says to him, with "this" designating a brand-new switchblade of his own, and divulging how proud this recent acquisition has made its owner.

Ti-Jus's friend keeps at him.

"Same as yours, almost. See . . . ? Hey, take a look . . . !"

Ti-Jus concedes not a word, not a glance, neither at the switchblade nor his friend; and when he finally does decide to speak, it is to announce tersely that he isn't free—something to do, a visit to Vallon, a delivery to make for his mother.

With poor articulation and falling intonation, as though—since the decision is a matter of course—there's no need to state it clearly or completely, the friend says, the first of two times, "I'm coming along." But learns that Ti-Jus intends to go by himself.

"Come on . . . !" the friend says, giving voice to his disappointment in the singsong extension of the second syllable—"Come aaaaan . . . !"—a disappointment tinged with surprise, even a certain disbelief: still clinging to a thread of hope, or merely the fond wish, that Ti-Jus must be just kidding.

Then the second time, but with a new intonation, straddling an uncomfortable middle ground between entreaty and decree:

"I'm coming along."

Ti-Jus confirms, "No." Explains: "Not with that knife on you, you're not."

At this, overcome by anger, or just by a vehemence that could pass for anger, the friend undergoes a complete change. In a face gone suddenly livid, his eyes shine with a blind incandescence, and the mass of his otherwise good-natured person turns electric. Peppering his speech with swearwords like *Arecaceae* or *three-hole suck-juice*, in a voice charged with petulance and rage, he agrees to the terms. He'll leave his switchblade here, okay, no big deal; he's going to leave it behind, his knife—and he repeats *okay*. Then, just like when we've gotten indignant and expect to receive a real dressing-down in return, to keep us from crossing that line again—something like "Don't ever say that to me again!"—Ti-Jus's friend reproves him for having initially refused outright instead of granting conditional consent, which would have been enough. He cites the meaning of the word *company*: Does Ti-Jus know the meaning of the word *company* . . . ? Which is what the friend is in his host's house? Doesn't he hear *panis* in the word, recalling the breaking of bread, and in *companion* too: "He who accompanies, who goes along" . . . ? So—and with index finger brandished, or both palms turned heavenward, and still swearing savagely—"Three-hole suck-juice!"—"without the switchblade" would have been enough. "You come along, because you are my companion, but without the switchblade," would have been enough. No need to explain why. Nor even to say whether or not Ti-Jus—Trisuckjuice!—would be keeping his own switchblade in his pocket.

Placid, indifferent to this performance, Ti-Jus, in the end, stands in front of his friend and stares at him, silent. Giving the impression that he might be reconsidering his decision. Perhaps he's wondering now just how much the presence of this third party might affect the unfolding of proximate future events, and how consequential it might prove for this same third party to have ventured into them in the first place. Then, all of a sudden, he extends his hand, while in the same neutral tone of voice he would have used to deliver not some personal preference, but a verdict of fate, says, "All right. Hand it over," or only "All right," or only "Hand it over." The friend complies, gratified though still somewhat unsettled. Ti-Jus takes the switchblade. His eyes elsewhere, his mind on other matters or already thinking through the next subject, he tosses the knife carelessly onto his bed, in among the jumble of a duvet half on the floor and a bedspread piled with audio cassettes.

When the two boys reappear in the living room, Bessie moves toward them, upright, elbows to her body, careful to keep her forearms perfectly parallel and horizontal beneath the long package she's carrying.

"Here," she begins. "Careful not to spoil . . ."

The sight of the slashed jeans stops her before *anything*.

"You're not going over there dressed like that, are you?"

Ti-Jus asks, "What do you mean, *like that*?"—to which Bessie doesn't dare, doesn't know, doesn't understand . . . She says, "Well, I don't know, I mean," then sighs: "Oh never mind, it doesn't matter . . . !"

She extends her arms, pointing with her chin to the square of paper pinned to the package.

"There's the address."

And in an attempted return to her earlier warning:

"Don't spoil anything!"

But, having been deferred, *spoil* and *anything* have both evolved; and though they are both words that ten minutes ago were intended to secure the package in the care of its deliverer, they are now charged with a new anxiety, and instead signify "My big boy!," "My little one!," or "My Ti-Jus!"; one or the other of these exclamations followed by "Please, I'm serious, stay out of trouble!"

Thus implored, and placed in charge of the package so carefully prepared by his mother, the son and his friend go on their way. They head down the three flights of stairs at top speed, filling the stairwell with the resounding vibrations of the steps they barely graze in passing. Conversely, as soon as they're through the automatic door on the ground floor and out in the open, as they move away toward the Vallon Apartments, the noise that all the machine tools and automobiles keep up all around them wholly absorbs the sounds of their steps; so that, at once conspicuous to the eye and nonexistent to the ear, they appear as strange pedestrians who, while necessarily making foot-contact with the ground, nevertheless seem to belong more to the air, or to the idea of the air, than to the asphalt, or the sensory world of their fellow men.

According to the law, but also to custom, and to common sense in either case, in order to reach their intended destination, they should have been walking down Beuilhet Way for two or three hundred meters. At the first crossing, they should have turned left to bypass the shopping center and gone to cross the Avenue de Paris via an underground passage. Once on the other side, they should again have taken a left and continued up the narrow road below avenue-level, walking first between embankment and building site, next between embankment and evergreen hedge, until arriving at a wide gap in the row of shrubs, punctuated on either end by two granite pillars, one of which is adorned with golden lettering that spells: *Vallon Apartments* . . . But this is not what they did. They opted for the rusticity of the straight line over the civility of the detour. They chose the bleakness of the broad vacant strip separating Avenue de Paris and the Mermoz Projects, the discomfort of slick, loamy soil strewn with rusty metal, glass shards, and animal excrement. Shortly thereafter, further emboldened, they will clamber over the guardrail and endeavor to weave their way across the blacktop, despite the uninterrupted flow of traffic wholly unprepared for this surprise incursion. Then there will be a mayhem of swerving; screeching brakes and screaming tires will be heard above car horns—after which, except for the rare stoics, the drivers involved will discharge their excess frustration, some shouting a vengeful insult through a car window lowered for just this purpose, others heaving a deep, sorrowful sigh, as if faced with some failed conciliation, or mumbling, "Smart, very smart," or "Little punks," shaking their heads with the look of smug disgust you find on the face of someone comforted in their own worst misanthropic convictions. All this notwithstanding, the two boys will refuse to run, or pick up their pace in the least. Just as they're about to reach the Vallon side of the road, the friend will turn around to address an erect and phallic finger to his fleeing public, while Ti-Jus, for his part, will continue on his haughty way, head raised, looking off into the distance, reacting neither to the voiced animosity behind him nor to the disheartened collective spirit of the motorists. He will hold the package in front of his chest, across his forearms, just as he would a young body rescued from death, or else chosen for sacrifice. And the jeans, jacket, and sweater he's wearing will impose their gaudy pigments on the landscape: sapphire blue—most precious of precious stones; heartbreak red—color of spilt blood; and yellow, too—color of the clayey earth after the first post-drought rains have fallen, making it gleam beneath our sandals with a brilliance akin to that produced by the varnished fronds and coconuts hovering over our heads . . . year in, year out.

1. 10

From their windows in the Mermoz Projects, several girls had been tracking the boys' progress, and with a considerably less maternal eye than Bessie's, which had also been following them at the same moment—but still keenly interested, roused in their own way by the spectacle of such a daring venture, watching for the moment when it would resolve into oblivion, and, during this wait, wondering whether the two solitary pedestrians were shrinking in proportion to their increased remoteness or to the approaching dusk.

A short while later, other girls, this time very young ones grouped as a threesome in front of the entrance to the Vallon Apartments, watched as the same two silhouettes appeared from on high, emerging from out of the galactic light produced by the giant candelabra that bordered the Avenue de Paris, just beginning to coat everything in their electric glare. The girls were carrying on a running commentary, speaking fast and laughing excitedly. Then, as the walkers approached, they quite conspicuously turned their backs, tightened their circle, and furtively carried on chatting, but in hushed tones.

Ti-Jus passed without paying any attention to the girlish clique, which provoked neither a smile nor a whistle from his friend—only a cursory glance. On the residential grounds, the lamps flanking the entrance to the two apartment buildings, as well as the outdoor lights scattered throughout the lawn, wooded areas, and private garden paths, had just come on. A woman at the wheel of her car was slowly approaching the exit, and straightened her back on seeing Ti-Jus, emphasizing her bust. A security guard was present as well: distrustful, zealous, unfriendly.

"Who do you want? Why?" he barked with each repetition of the name Fenerolo.

He insisted on accompanying the carrier and his acolyte to the rear apartment building, then hurried ahead to take up a position in front of the intercom before they could reach it.

"Deux-Rivières, a package. Accompanied by another young person . . . Yes? Are you sure?"

He preceded the visitors into the lobby, wiping his feet with exemplary thoroughness on the large doormat, while squinting into the mirrors on either side, as if to make sure no assailants were lurking. Reassured, and deeming his mission to be complete, or else feeling reluctant to act any further against the grain of his autarchic tendencies, he pointed to the elevator and walked out, without waiting for the doors to open obligingly for this pair of weary riders, come from so far away.

Floor 1, then 2, 3, 4, and 5 appearing on the display, the elevator door once again—and then the door to the manager's apartment—opened to the new arrivals. Not the slightest hint of hostility or reticence on the part of the carrier. His friend, unobtrusive. "Come in, come in!" Madame Fenerolo announced, and eventually, "Hello, how nice of you to come all this way!"—and, reacting to the package: "Ah, wonderful!"

She preceded the young men into the living area and offered them a seat anywhere on the living-room side, while she branched off toward the bar counter that divided the room in half. Would they have a beer? A Coke?

No thanks, Ti-Jus had just had something to drink, his friend as well.

"Nuceeef!" conceded the latter, impressed at once by the comfort of the chair he'd been offered, by the décor of the apartment, and finally by the valley outside, bathed in the last blaze of sunset, as seen through the picture windows; impressed too by the pleasant smile, V-neck sweater, and unexpectedly attractive figure of the lady of the house.

For she was indeed smiling, Madame Fenerolo, and pleasantly: a model of harmonious congeniality, no doubt about it, in her straight skirt and under her V-neck sweater; and what's more, she was no less a manager then, that evening, than at any other time—no less manager at home than at Bessie's, in her Opel, at the SUMABA, or anywhere else in Île-de-France.

"So, let's have a look, shall we?" she said, coming back toward the two boys.

Ti-Jus handed her the package. She asked him to put it down there—adding immediately, "Wait," as she arranged the magazines that had been scattered around the living-room table into a stack—which he did, before moving just to one side to take up position, standing expectantly, his weight shifting slightly onto one leg, two times four fingers in his hip pockets. He sniffed. He lifted his right hand to his nostrils, rubbed them with his wrist, lowered it, and finally let it dangle in front of his thigh, thumb inserted into the upper slash in his jeans.

Outside, a car was slowly maneuvering between the front and rear buildings. Its tires were making a continuous unsticking sound on the asphalt, or else a dull crackling on the fine gravel; a sound, in either case, that could in no way compare with the silky, heartrending rasp that such tires would have produced on sand . . . The manager was about to say something.

"While we're at it, I'll just . . ."

And with that, she began a gesture, leaving it unfinished, her right hand resting on the bracelet encircling her left wrist. Then, seeming now to have made a firmer decision, instead of bending her knees and sitting back on her heels, as she had been about to do in order to open the package, she turned around, walked a few steps away, stating that she was going to entrust Ti-Jus with a check—and then changing her mind once again.

"Oh . . . well . . . Actually, I'll just settle this with your mom tomorrow."

Her gaze settled on Ti-Jus's face, and he in return showed no sign of caring whether or not his face or demeanor pleased her: no sign of feeling, no sign of any thought whose object was present in the room. In a flash, the manager might have concluded that there was a certain remote place that, geographically or otherwise, was occupying the better part of the young man's mind and senses. Perhaps she was intrigued, even envious of this place . . . A restrained impulse left her suspended. Her own hand, as if aspiring to some secret repose, had slipped softly into the neckline of her sweater to wind up enclosing her bare shoulder.

She was quick to recover her composure, however, and then, back at the package, Madame Fenerolo pointed purposefully at Ti-Jus's blue jeans, the slashes near the upper tibia and along the groin where his right-hand thumb was hooked into position. "All those holes," she said. "Is that on purpose . . . ? Must get awfully drafty in there! And in this weather too! Aren't you freezing?"

Ti-Jus kept quiet. Unwavering, and likewise unhurried, he walked around the living-room table; having now inserted himself between coffee table and female body, he crouched down.

"I'll open it," he said, already opening the package.

Silence in the living room, apart from the tearing of the adhesive tape, then the unfolding and crumpling of the kraft paper. Ti-Jus said, "There." Though he lingered before moving aside, getting up.

"You have to try them on."

He was quiet for another moment—but still without getting up or turning to the manager. And then:

"My mother would like you to try them on."

1. 11

Looking surprised, mildly amused, a hint of irony in her voice, before saying, "All right," Madame Fenerolo asked, "Now?" And then, more seriously:

"I'll be just a minute."

She's crossed the living room to seek the privacy of her bedroom, carrying the mended skirt and new pantsuit across her arm. Ti-Jus hasn't budged. In his friend's mind, by way of monologue, that single word, *Nucif*, the *i* variously elongated, keeps recurring—or else *holes-suck-juice* or *Palmae* . . . across a whole range of intonations. The incessant stop-start of the elevator in the hall, the sound of voices or a ringing telephone heard through the walls and floors—noises of this kind create a buffer zone between the apartment and the outside world; a world, indistinguishable from the distant sound of traffic on the Avenue de Paris, belonging to an inaccessible time and space, with no connection whatsoever to time and space as experienced by the two waiting adolescents, or by Madame Fenerolo in the process of removing her straight skirt. The friend sits slumped down contemptuously in his chair, knees at eye-level, feet flat on the carpet. His position remains unchanged, but the look of contempt on his face fades each time his involuntarily darting gaze meets that of Ti-Jus. In her room, the manager has opened a wardrobe. In the living room, Ti-Jus has stood back up. She extends a hand to reach a toiletries bag, a purse, or to open a jewelry box. Ti-Jus says to his friend, "Don't move," or "Stay here." She slips hangers along a rod, pushing several aside before choosing the one holding a camisole, belonging to some matching panty and camisole set. Ti-Jus exits the living room, walks down the hall; she hears him approaching. Then, experiencing the twin impulse of turning her head toward the door and clutching the hanger and camisole to her breast, she freezes, until Ti-Jus, though he's already entered the room and shut the door behind him, asks if he can come in.

Out on the Avenue de Paris, traffic continues, unabated, having forgotten the recent disruption by two reckless teens, and unaware of what exists, of what might be going on beyond the guardrails that channel its flow. Ti-Jus's friend explores the living-room, making himself at home now that he's alone. He dishevels the pile of magazines distractedly, fiddles with a few bibelots, rummages through a drawer, helps himself to the contents of the mini fridge in the bar. Or he just wriggles in his chair, constantly shifting in his seat and drumming on its armrests with his phalanges. Or, again, having advanced to the threshold of the hallway, he listens intently to the noises coming from the bedroom . . . Despite his instructions to the contrary, does he intend to get closer to the ongoing events, or even take part in them himself . . . ? His inner voice continually repeats and parses *Palmae, Nucif,* and *holes-suck-juice,* which beckon other slang terms that assemble and proliferate in turn, accumulating and merging, stimulating nerve centers in such a way as to arouse a new movement here, a new posture there—a bending of the spine, a tossing back and forth of the head in disbelief, an opening of the mouth, scraps of aborted laughter then making their escape . . .

In the bedroom, meanwhile, shadows cast by a lampshade imprint their streaks onto the bedspread, broken up by darkness before extending vertically onto one of the doors of the wardrobe, still wide open. The shadows also leave their stamp on the sweater, the T-shirt, the velvety nape of Ti-Jus's neck as he raises his head; on his face, sheltered till now in the twilight of bodies face to face. The icy draft filtering through the slightly-open window and the warm air pulsating from the convection heater, as well as the fumes of female camphoric cologne and male aftershave, at times merging, at others floating along in parallel, all diverge and converge in accordance with the tiny barometric variations and movements in the room—arms pulling, feet pushing, fingers that loosen their grip only to grab on higher up, fingers grown numb by the tightness of their grasp, no longer able to feel whether they're clutching at a soft or rough surface, flat or convex, smooth or uneven . . . Ti-Jus employs unbridled force, alternatively bending and unbending his posture, as though wanting to move forward, or else lift himself along the body that his embrace has overpowered, while the steep arch of his back and the tensing of his muscles lend bulk to his silhouette. This additional density calls upon abdominals and adductors as much as biceps and pectorals; and yet, more than any other part of his body, of the surface of his skin, he is compressing the palms of his hands, which are overheating, blazing, especially after slipping slightly, or, when shifting their grasp, they then recover their hold with a violent slapping sound.

Since Ti-Jus entered, with his "Can I come in?," the manager hasn't said a word, or in any way made her voice heard. At most, and at intervals, she has let out an isolated syllable or mere consonant, followed by nothing, or, even less articulated and exteriorized, by a kind of involuntary humming, strictly organic, unconscious, and as foreign to language as the beating of rain on palm stipes or the whistling of wind through pinnate leaves.

This limited vocal production is not to his liking, is insufficient for Ti-Jus, who wants instead to hear *stipe* and *pinnate* repeated, then *the beating of rain on stipes*, and *the whistling of wind through pinnate leaves*. The manager refuses to comply, turns her head, her face in profile and silent for a few moments, before at last yielding to the insistence of the one who now wants to hear her say *copra*—she says "copra"—*tar and copra*—she says "tar and copra." He wants to hear *wet sand* and *dry sand*. He wants *palisade*. He wants *roof, detachable doors, detachable shutters*, and, more, wants *lobster trap, mat, basket, fan* or indeed any other noun designating an item that can be made out of all or part of the pinnate leaf of the coconut palm after it dries and changes color. And while he continues rising, advancing, lifting himself by the strength of his arms and legs, she repeats, nearly breathless now, "shutter," and "fan," and "lobster trap," and "mat," and "palisade," and "roof," and everything that Ti-Jus wants her to say.

He's going to kill her.

With the sharp yet unctuous click of a flawless spring mechanism and tempered steel, the switch releases its blade. The friend in the hallway immediately thinks, "He's killing her." He listens to what follows, as reluctant to move closer to the room as he is to pull back, wondering exactly what varieties of act are producing the new noises that are reaching his ears: like coir fibers torn from a husk, or the tearing of fabric, a violent blow, an object falling with a heavy thud. He also hears the security guard's griping and peals of brazen laughter from the girls they saw on their way into the residence . . . The girls' laughter, the guard's complaints, their respective footsteps or shuffling—these various noises stand out against the continuo of the cars, isolated in their own foreground, and yet diluted in the same night that now extends in all directions.

Back at the Mermoz Projects, an identical phenomenon allows music wafting from a car radio to be heard in the Deux-Rivières apartment, along with the muffled hubbub of kids gathered on the street of Beuilhet Way. To flee the noise, or simply because she feels a sudden, overwhelming need to be in motion, Bessie leaves the kitchen and joins her husband, who is once again indulging in his compulsive habit of pacing around the living room. But neither forbearance nor routine make any difference this evening: Bessie can't stand to watch Celestin going round in circles like that, bandy-legged—his arm subjected as ever to some invisible traction, his fingers clutching at who knows what . . . A bit sharply, she asks him to stop, only to immediately retract the request with an "I'm sorry" or "Don't mind me, I don't know what's wrong with me today." She blames the dreariness of late afternoon, her nerves, the prospect of another day of work at the SUMABA.

Homeward bound at last, Ti-Jus and his friend plunge wordlessly into the suburban night, puny shadows despite their size, as stunted as we ourselves might appear in other climes, when we go walking along the shore, exiting stage left, under the gaze of the coconut palms. Then, although we have disappeared, the trees remain in the company of the landscape that had contained us along with them, surrounded by the pungent odors generated by the heat and humidity, and which shall remain our scents forever, among the sounds that are the voices of the trees: the grazing of crab claws on sand, of lizards on tree trunks; a flapping of wings, the breaking of waves.

2. The Cargo Ship

2.01

As four hours Universal Time approaches, which in February is three o'clock Ris time, no harbinger of a new dawn emerges, but instead there is a deepening of night in the outlying suburbs. Not a sound to be heard. Nothing stirring. The nocturnal fog soaks the suburban lamplight, so that everywhere the same stagnant icy gray medium reigns, where earth and sky mingle, engulfing structures, sleepers, and vegetation alike. Should the odd rumbling be heard in the distance, there's no doubt that it must come from a jetliner, or the ground transport of some massive piece of precast concrete, a chunk of fuselage, or a blast-furnace tuyere—the noise is far off, in any case, either airborne or plausibly telluric, and its fading echo leaves a more leaden silence behind in the failed world.

And so it would seem that the only event capable of reviving space and lifting the suspension of time is a sudden, violent catastrophe. Instead, the event in question occurs slowly, gradually, as do all incidents requiring so supremely protracted an effort to wrench themselves free from inertia. Alone among thousands of dark windows in Île-de-France, one on an upper floor of an apartment building lights up. Fifteen kilometers away, an alarm clock goes off. Elsewhere, a gate creaks, or slams, sheet metal humming a moment before silence reigns once more. Another alarm clock sounds. The red glow of a cigarette in Joinville-le-Pont responds to that of a brazier being stoked in the chill of a vacant lot somewhere near

Pompadour Crossing. Another window lights up, while the headlights of a pickup truck sweep three billboards at a bend in the road in Rocquencourt . . . Yet, whether movement, light, or sound, each disturbance is infinitesimal; and although, with each passing minute, their number and frequency increase, they still hardly make a dent in the vast, almost solid, Île-de-France night.

One has to wait for the first planes to begin their approach maneuvers in the invisible skies over Roissy or Orly, then the first trains, the first Traffic Watch helicopters, and, joining the chorus, the roaring crescendo of automobile traffic, in order for the atmospheric space to grow slowly distinct from terra firma, and for the land, though as yet untouched by any hint of dawn, to begin stirring in its usual slow, copious palpitation. Here it swells with cars amassed at an intersection, there it ebbs where an esplanade is devoid of traffic; further on, it swells with pedestrians leaving a train station, there it ebbs when a car radio shuts off; further on, yet again, it swells with a gaggle of chattering voices, or the bidirectional movement of two regional express trains, and then ebbs elsewhere with the opening of an iron gate and the disappearance of the workers who were waiting in front of that gate, or with the return of silence on a railroad platform after a train's departure. Soon, the gap between the level of noise and motion attained on the roadways and the silent stillness that continues to reign in certain half-deserted zones of the landscape will have reached a maximum dispersion, such that seen from Ris-Orangis, from Champ-sur-Marne, or from Cergy-Pontoise, it might feel as though the very fabric of the region is about to unravel, to rip, to rend. Yet nothing of the sort happens. At very most, the movements of a few emergency vehicles set off a rippling motion at certain intervals, climaxing in a burst of sirens and rotating lights. Then, as though driven by the force of two opposing gusts of air, the congestions dissolve, become increasingly concentrated on the outskirts of Paris, scattered around the provincial edges, while the night gradually gives way to an overcast day, as foretold in the previous evening's weather report, looking much the same now as it will throughout the rest of the day, and until nightfall, unchanging.

In that daylight, or even before day breaks on the A6 Highway between Longjumeau and Fresnes, the hulking frames of two thirty-five-ton rigs tower over the gridlock. Traffic is creeping. Forward motion occurs sporadically over four nonsynchronous lanes, so that the two trucks are alternately neck and neck or separated by several meters . . . tens of meters, at times. When they happen to meet alongside, the two drivers strike up a kind of dialogue. First by signs—looks exchanged along with shruggings of shoulders, brows arched in resignation, torsos pushed back, palms turned conspicuously upward. Now, one of the drivers has lowered his window to say hello to his fellow trucker, who, after sliding laterally across his front seat, returns the greeting, his upper body leaning obliquely toward the right, his left arm stretched to the limit in the other direction, leaving only his fingertips to keep contact with the steering wheel.

The first driver asks: "You familiar with this area?" and the other, with an immediately perceptible foreign accent despite the shortness of his answer, replies "Huh?"

"Go ahead, go ahead," says the native, since the cars behind them are honking now in exasperation, urging the second driver to inch forward.

The conversation resumes further down the road, a little later, lasting longer this time thanks to the two center lanes having inexplicably ground to a complete halt, while the trucks, reunited now at the same latitude, watch as cars speed past them in both the outside lanes.

"Are you familiar," the native repeats, "with . . ."—and this time supplies some more specifics—"Bagneux," "SUMABA." He explains he has a delivery to make there.

Giving no evidence of having understood a word, the second driver simply repeats, in his own way, "Are you familiar," as well as "SUMABA," before signifying via gesticulation and facial expression that, despite the patently Parisian license plates mounted in back of his rig, he doesn't speak any French. In his own language, he adds something that the native driver in turn fails to understand. The native is stumped: what language is this? Who is this fellow hauler . . . ? Resigned to leaving these questions unanswered, resigned likewise to being unable to obtain any tips from the non-French trucker as to the best route for getting to Bagneux, he nonetheless continues to question him, with a friendly "Paris?"

And without waiting for a reply, tries a more explicit formulation:

"Are you going to Paris?"

Still not giving up:

"You? Paris?"

He's speaking loudly now, left hand cupped as megaphone, not because his listener is all that far away, but because the native's words have to wend their way against the immensity of the sky, against the remnants of the nocturnal gloom and the icy winter damp that hovers between the sheer cliffs of the two trucks. The non-French speaker is disconcerted. He repeats, abstrusely, "Paris?"—then proceeds to raise the same word an octave, overjoyed all of a sudden, nodding madly: yes, yes, yes.

Separated by random shifts in traffic, the two truckers exchange complicit looks and smiles via the side-view mirror of the forward-most truck. Reunited once more, they lower their windows to the cold fog mixed with exhaust fumes, and to the raucous commotion of roaring motors, shuddering bodywork, and radios leaking music. They converse. Or, with windows closed, one driver having pointed to the dial of his watch with a cynical smirk, the other plays along, adding a Gallic poking of his inflated cheek with his index finger. Or, again, displaying a high level of technical prowess amid this otherwise casual encounter, each driver busies himself about his cabin, relinquishes his steering wheel on the least pretense, practically standing up, turning his back to the dashboard to grab some object or place it on his berth, thereby multiplying the number of non-essential actions being undertaken, as though to prove to his colleague how easy, how second-nature, in fact, are the exigencies of their shared profession.

Because they're approaching—at a crawl, but approaching nonethe-less—the FRESNES exit where he'll have to get off the highway, the native lowers his window one last time. With a "Hey!" or a "Ho!," he calls out to his fellow driver. He makes him a gift of a porno magazine.

"Here," he says, face into the wind and arm extended over the void.

His colleague shows delight at the sight of the cover. He exclaims something and starts laughing before jutting out a grateful connoisseur's thumbs-up. Then, after hastily digging into his pockets, he extends his arm, offering a pack of cigarettes to his comrade, who greets this gift with a drawn-out "oh yeah."

When the first truck has started lumbering into the exit lane, once its driver has engaged its front-wheel axle, gradually steering the length of his vehicle into the right-hand lane—once, finally, he's hauled out onto the sloping curve of the exit ramp—the ever-widening gap between the two giant rigs is revealed, appearing immaculate, fresh, as though it's been sheltered for ages from all light and air. The pristine gap spreads, un-hurried. Little by little, it gains horizontality, bringing with it the sounds of morning, wafting low over the suburbs, with nothing to impede its steady progress except perhaps during the time it takes for a truck horn to sound thrice, doubled by its echo—followed then by a short honk, and *its* echo—the blaring baritone adieus called out from afar by the two truckers.

2. 02

In front of the SUMABA, the security guard's dog—only just taken off its leash—has hurled itself into the parking lot, exhaling plumes of breath into the surrounding fog and darting around every which way; then, having stopped to piss against the north fence, it's resumed its zigzagging, less feverishly now, muzzle no longer sniffing the wind but quivering at blacktop level, in search of new, fragrant discoveries, or else sweet memories.

With a sextupled whistle, the guard has called it back—or, else, calling it by name, "Bucco," shouting twice: "Bucco! Bucco! . . ."

Bathed in the orangey light that the gray dawn and raw highway glare manage both to bleach and sully, man and dog are reflected in the plate-glass doors of the supermarket: caught in the same gleaming transparency, and as bereft of their physical substance as the shopping carts that shine in the foreground beneath their concrete canopy, the lampposts staked into the parking-lot blacktop, and, all the way in the background, the five or six SUMABA delivery vans parked by the western fence. The dog's frenzy and sparse movements of its master serve only to highlight the stillness of the place, which will nonetheless come gradually alive as the population in its vicinity grows dense, and busies itself with various activities. The daytime security and the meat-counter staff will be arriving first. They'll greet the truck from the slaughterhouse whose white-hooded crew will unload the day's fresh carcasses. Next, the store warehouse workers, delivery drivers, floor staff, and supplies manager will be arriving, individually or by twos and threes, some in cars, others on motorcycles or bikes, still others on foot from the bus or train station . . . But, this morning, between "fresh carcasses" and "Next," the ground begins to quake, shaking all the nearby lampposts, plate glass, and grillwork. Bucco the dog stands stock still, ears pricked. The night watchman and the daytime security guards, the meat-counter staff in their civvies, and the slaughterhouse people in white overcoats all pause as well. Beneath the soles of their feet, as well as deep inside their leg bones, they are experiencing vibrations whose cause can't be perceived by eye or ear; and several seconds pass like this before they begin to hear an unidentifiable rumble, muted and continuous, and then several more seconds pass before they begin to make out the arrival and then gradual enlargement of a certain glow beaming through the screen of foggy half-light in front of them. Then, glow and rumble combined take shape, become radiator grill, become truck. And only then does the entire vehicle emerge, move forward, colossal and cautious, as though taking great pains, even feeling regret, needing now to return to the visible world after so protracted an isolation in the ghostly realms.

After maneuvering into place, after parking, cutting the motor, and unloading his cargo, the trucker heads over to the supplies manager's office, paperwork in hand. All the supermarket's indoor lighting has been switched on now. Already half-inhabited, still half-deserted, the building resonates with the sound of comings and goings, of conversations, and of pre-opening prep work, such as stacking cans, decorating a display case, changing price tags, or supplying the end caps with the least recent arrivals. A man and woman in white smocks are in the process of setting up a mixed delicatessen display. The male of the duo, noting the arrival of a car in the parking lot, wonders whether it might be Madame Fenerolo—but seeing that it isn't, he says aloud, "No it isn't. It's . . ." followed by three female first names. And indeed, three women, three cashiers, pile out of the car, two of whom rush to enter the store while the third, despite the cold, joins the group that's formed around the giant truck. She's greeted with "Morning," and "Hi"; someone goes "You see this?" along with a tilt of the head to designate, generally speaking, what there is to see—or else a finger pointing more specifically towards a headlight, a set of lug nuts, the multicolored pennants lined up in a garland along the side of the hood, or the airfoil set atop the cabin, curved into an elbow-shape like the intake duct on a ship. The cashier is also shown the wheels, five pairs, three of which are doubled, making sixteen wheels altogether—sixteen wheels, sixteen wheels as big as this one, can you imagine?

The cashier repeats "sixteen wheels," admiring, unquestioning; she repeats "sixteen wheels," emphasizing the *six*; or, huddled in her coat, arms crossed protectively across her chest and face still swollen with sleep, she makes do with mumbling, a sub-audible whistle, or a nod of the head.

One of the supply men expresses surprise that a vehicle this size would be allowed on the local two-lane Fontenay Road. A second supply man, a truculent sort, looking for a fight, counters the claim. He disputes whether the Fontenay road is in fact a local two-lane, whether the truck really needs all that much room anyway. I mean, did you see how it nailed the turn! How it just eased into place! . . . It seems for a moment that the dispute will end there, but then, with intensified animosity, the second supply man goes on the offensive. He starts off with: "These tanks! . . ." Then, just as one might heft a switchblade in one's hand by way of warning, or lash the air with it in a series of mock attacks, he lays out his argument with "super power steering," "easier than a car," "with one finger" . . . The first supply man beats a retreat. On principle, he snickers—"Easy, my ass!"—but his eyes are shifty, his voice muffled, insecure; and, eager to forget, or have the others forget this altercation, he affects a retreat into contemplation, monologuing under his breath: "A beautiful beast, no doubt about it," or "One hell of a body."

The upper part of the truck gleams impeccably. But the lower part is filthy, plastered with soot and spackled with mud deposited over many kilometers. Though no one says anything about it, the dirt conjures up images of slick roads, icy patches, of sand, of water, of salt, and unending trepidation . . . Then a grumpy voice intervenes to predict that by tonight, the trucker will have logged quite a few kilometers more, will probably have changed coordinates several times. As he speaks, the grump withdraws his hand from his pocket, a calloused hand, fingers so stumpy they can't fully bend or stretch; and as he extends his arm toward the northeastern horizon, his companions all follow his gesture, fully expecting to discover—against all optical logic—a view of Picardie hovering at the end of his crooked index finger, and beyond Picardie, Hainaut, and further on, Brabant, Anvers, North Brabant . . .

But when word comes of Madame Fenerolo's arrival, general attention turns from these fantastic visions and the sight of the thirty-five-ton rig. The manager steps onto the parking lot blacktop. She shouts "Hello everybody!" while turning around to get her pelisse from off the back seat. She stands back up and locks the four doors of her Opel with the remote-control keychain.

"Has the meat been delivered?"

They assure her it has. Yes, the slaughterhouse truck has just left—but what about this one here: has she ever seen anything so beautiful, so enormous?

Madame Fenerolo concedes that the thirty-five ton rig is indeed beautiful and enormous—but without emotion, not entirely won over, her mind obviously on what she's about to say, not on what she's just said:

"The shopping carts . . ."

She raises her voice so as to be heard at a distance: they didn't all have to be put inside that way; leave half of them—no, that's too many, a third, leave a third inside, that should be enough; a third inside, the rest outside . . . okay?

2. 03

When Bessie arrives at the SUMABA in turn, she watches from the parking lot as the silhouette of the thirty-five-ton rig—several kilometers away now—glides imperceptibly toward the horizon. She also sees a helicopter sailing over the suburb, alone in the whitish sameness of the sky where it flies unobstructed in the same direction as the thirty-five-ton rig. The aircraft shrinks, slows down, and descends, or seems to descend, until it almost touches the truck, hovering in place, or at least adjusting its speed to match that of the behemoth, hanging above it for a long while; then, pulling away all of a sudden, it regains its former altitude and speed, curves around, and heads straight back for Bagneux.

"Hello, TWC!" calls the crew. "This is Dragonfly, this is Dragonfly. Over."

Her back turned to the SUMABA, Bessie watches both the helicopter drawing nearer and the thirty-five-ton rig continuing to recede into the distance. She's cold, thinks she would feel better inside the store, and anyway, it's time she tended to her cash register. And yet she stays outside, in the same pose assumed by anyone indulging in a daydream while still staring at the quotidian world, the same pose assumed as well by the people watching from shore as we cast off—they stand on the wharf while the pilot boat brings back the marine pilot who guided us out of the harbor, as our cargo ship heads out to sea . . . Those of us on board have already lost interest in the coastline that pitches off stern and dwindles, engrossed as we are—not by the sea, but by our own sense of balance and by our movements now instinctively adjusting to the instability of the gangways, to the narrowness of the ladder rungs or the verticality of the handrails, while those people back on dry land, watching, unsure whether they envy or pity us, will have to endure the pangs of separation for much longer than ourselves.

The day goes by, managerial for the manager, nothing but cash registers and bar codes for the cashier. By the time the SUMABA closes, it's already nightfall. The silhouettes of the employees scatter. The parking lot is practically empty. From thirty meters away, Madame Fenerolo shouts to Bessie, who's waiting by the metallic gray Opel: "I'll be right there, Bessie." Then, as the two women wind their way from Bagneux to Ris-Orangis, there is talk of which route to take—"by way of Fontenay"—of foul weather—"Here comes the rain"—of place of residence and daytime hours—"You like Ris too, don't you?"—and "You'd never know the days were getting longer . . ." Also discussed is the pantsuit being tailored at the Mermoz Projects, as well as the wraparound skirt with the lining that shows below the hem—"Look, Bessie"—appearing against a background of see-through pantyhose, between the knees and thighs of Madame Fenerolo at the wheel.

At the point when the A106 and the N7 become closed to traffic, the Opel is still on the Bagneux surface road. The car has reached Fresnes by the time the rain starts, and then Thiais, when, infuriated, the manager switches off the radio. Muddled by the sweep of the wipers, trembling and creeping in unruly slabs across the windshield, the water creates a vision of a landscape where form and void have grown indistinguishable, and where the sky, rather than allowing space to expand, has clamped it shut beneath a dark, flat, aqueous surface. Thus, the distant aerial beacons and blinking airplane lights look like aquatic mirages, while at surface level, the evening fog, mingling with exhaust fumes in the steady effervescent rebound of rain, cushions the blacktop with a cloud pierced here and there by the sidereal brilliance of headlights and the lunar glow of streetlamps.

In the shelter of their cars, or at home, thousands of *Franciliens* are watching the water pour out of the sky, then watching the sky-water transmute into hail. A phenomenon like this never fails to engross. It saturates the ear, rendering all speech futile. It sets the nerves on edge . . . In fact, inside the Opel, idle chatter has given way to a highly charged silence. The same holds true at the Deux-Rivières household, where, behind the openwork kitchen curtains, Celestin has stiffened. He, whose tilt of the head toward his shoulder had until now expressed nothing more than listlessness, nostalgia, unease, or affliction, now tenses his jaws and clenches his fists . . . While, back in the car, Madame Fenerolo recovers her voice.

"And that big boy of yours," she asks, "what does he want to do?"

Or, as if among family:

"And what about that Ti-Jus?"

Then, having learned which vocation the young man is considering in his spare time, after a fleeting moment of dismay, she displays effusive approval. She posits what a big world it is out there, alludes to the powerful call of those distant horizons—apparently feeling no shame at saying "big world," or "call of those distant horizons." Her breathing quickens, she raises her face, giving a sort of depth to her gaze; as though, in a sudden, fervent impulse towards frankness, she were in fact speaking of her own personal ideal. But abruptly changing the subject:

"It'll be nice, don't you think, Bessie, a seafood counter?"

Within the question itself, and before it's even formulated in the manager's mouth, breath and saliva have already bound together the words and their effect—the tongue has rolled *it* together with *it*, *will be* with *will be*, *nice* with *nice*, and *yes* with each word up to *counter*. Acquiescence is thus formed in advance. It has already ripened in the humid warmth of Madame Fenerolo's mouth. And then, expelled from the bounds of this orifice by the utterance of what both contained and solicited it, acquiescence emerges from *Bessie*, from *don't think*, from *you*. So that here it is, still virtual, yet fully assembled and ready for use, prowling around the closed compartment of the metallic gray Opel, amid the mingled scents of its two occupants and an ambient air temperature set at just over 72°F. Convinced it's right: "Yes, it will be nice." It takes its time . . . or, worse, tinged with enthusiasm: "Oh yes! That'll be nice! . . ." It hardly matters that the willful spirit the utterance is putting under siege might only have wanted to greet it with resignation . . . or that this spirit might perhaps have wanted to resist. And even if we were to beseech it—"If only, if only Bessie wouldn't . . ." or "Please, at least let Bessie be granted permission to say nothing!"—it would take no notice, calmly committing its violence.

Thus, when Bessie finally does acquiesce, it amounts to an atrocity.

2. 04

Paris, like the suburbs, had experienced its moment of hail. Right from the first few seconds, it sounded as though icy machine-gun pellets were going to shoot through car hoods, shatter windshields and glass canopies, rip through awnings. Cars all came to a halt, and when unable to find haven in the scant space of some bus shelter, or else take refuge in the metro, pedestrians huddled under porch canopies and cornices, as stunned by the sudden strangeness of the urban landscape around them as they were by the frenetic humming of the hailstones.

The sky having changed back to a less solid state, traffic resumed. Shelters emptied out. Once again, the city resounded with its usual driving, walking, rush hour garrulousness. One street, however, or a section of street, in the Quinze-Vingts neighborhood, was slow to return to normal. No vehicles were crowding the road, except for the ones that were parallel parked; no engines were revving up for departure; no cars turning onto this street from elsewhere, despite the opportunity it offered motorists to bypass the intersection at Boulevard Diderot and Rue de Lyon. Even pedestrians were rare, and those few present were widely scattered, heads under hoods or umbrellas. Nevertheless, from anonymous bystander to anonymous bystander, there soon manifested a desire for contact. Looks were exchanged, signifying "So you noticed it, too?" or "Weird, wasn't it?" Smiles of denied anxiety began to show through their worried looks:

a fleeting phenomenon, as though the usual inertia slowing all urban hustle and bustle to an irritable crawl had now solidified entirely, bringing people to a complete halt; an event portending nothing in particular; an effect disproportionate to its cause—they weren't alone, in any case. Indeed, little by little, the people still displaying their usual indifference, forcing themselves forward, became the exception. Only a few pensive passersby held out, their eyes glued to the sidewalk immediately upstream from their next footstep—a few particularly busy people who never broke stride as they searched their pockets or talked on their phones. But eventually, even these shared in the common sentiment. The question "What's going on?" was now displayed on every face, made manifest by every body. Left unanswered, the question evolved into "Is there something brewing?," then "Will it be something serious?," and then "Where will it come from?" They watched the skies, as though fearful it might rain down acid or salt, corrupting the waters of the earth. Ears pricked up in expectation of the unlikeliest sounds from neighboring streets: weeping and wailing, mooing, crying and croaking, all of which would reach a pitch testifying to the most unspeakable agonies, or even an overall regression of the species itself. Here on this block in the Quinze-Vingts neighborhood, fate had temporarily spared a few specimens of a dying race—but not for long. Chirring clouds of locust, then blue-black bolts of venomous bluebottle flies, and anopheles mosquitoes, were all going to pour out of the darkening sky, invading everything, devouring everything, poisoning everything; or perhaps, out of sight, millions of killer bacteria were already at work on people's flesh . . . A lamplight flickered, and all eyes immediately converged on it. An omen of the darkness to come . . . ? The shared dream of possible emergency rescue teams caused some to experience a short burst of hope, while for others, it was a sign of how bad things had already gotten. No one moved.

And just then, wonder of wonders, though not yet moving forward, nor indeed appearing as though they'd ever stirred from that spot, Ti-Jus and his three friends appeared at the far northern end of the street.

They took up the entire breadth of the street. All in profile, identically, the friends let their eyes wander over the façades stage right as though looking for some kind of peace of mind, a nervous release, a relaxation of the muscles before springing into action. One of them was smoking. Ciggy clinging to one lip, he paid no heed to the rain—or else was defying it—his young, ascetic face turned up into the weather, into the vertical beams of the streetlamp. Behind him, the hulk with the comb rocked lazily from one foot to the other, while the third friend, left hand extended obliquely toward the ground, snapped his fingers to the rhythm of a lullaby. Ti-Jus, alone, his hair pearled with droplets, then turned his back to the street that the foursome's sudden appearance had left speechless. He stood at a slight distance from his friends, arms brought symmetrically forward, legs straight, feet spread: the pissing boy position.

Whether insult, warning, or joke, a phrase shouted by the third friend elicited a no-less equivocal and resounding echo from the ascetic smoker, then a remark full of smug hilarity from the hulk with the comb. The three boys said *bakker* instead of *back her*. They shortened *boatswain* into *bosun* or into simply *bos*, just as *Ti-Jus* became *Teejay* or *Teej* and *motherfucker* became *muff*.

"Let fly, muff, let fly!"

They spoke of *lining the windlass*, of *stowing* and *slackening the hawser*.

"Hey, Teejay. Need some crew over there, or what?"

"All scuppers open! . . ."

The people watched them without reacting, listened without saying a word, cowering in the face of the unpredictable, horrified at recognizing their own language in the argot being spoken, and yet understanding nothing.

2. 05

After turning back to the street, Ti-Jus fell nonchalantly into line with his three friends. Seemingly unconcerned by the rainwater streaming down his face and along his neck before disappearing into the soaking collar of his cloth jacket, he tossed his head back and, mouth wide, drank in the droplets, while at the same time rubbing his hands together, unhurriedly, lightly, palm and fingers against palm and fingers. Such a peaceful gesture should have attested to a good-natured disposition, just as the young man's tall, slim figure and fine features could have been read, in some other context, as an assurance of civility; but due to the cold, or some vehement emotion, the boy was intermittently racked from head to foot by a shiver; racked to such a degree that, far from providing reassurance, his exposed carotid artery, his gaping mouth, his eyes cast heavenward, and his dripping face all prompted those assembled—his captive audience—to wonder whether Ti-Jus was in the grip of voiceless ecstasy, or whether, on the verge of entering a trance state, he was going to suddenly lash out and indulge in the most savage of acts.

Time elapsed, nonetheless, without any forward motion on the boys' part, nor the outbreak of any crisis more serious than the trajectory of the smoking friend's discarded cigarette. This member of the group had aimed at a parked delivery van, where his ejected cigarette landed with a bounce, already extinguished by the rain. Or, alternatively, with a calculated flick, he sent the still-lit cigarette butt flying: the projectile landed in a freefall after completing a brief arc; the fall was endless; it felt like forever before the moment of impact, which would also mean the extinction of the glowing ash in the oily, iridescent water on the pavement . . . As if asking for an encore, or in order to applaud the feat, the hulk with the comb spat on the ground, and the third friend gave out a whistle, loud and long, twice in a row, lips narrowed, rolled over his teeth, half-devoured. Ti-Jus, on the other hand, shook the water from his hair and started his forward march, and his three friends likewise fell into step.

Each at his own pace, on his own course, lively or sluggish, staccato, even-keeled, more or less tortuous. Only one moved straight forward, with large, weighty strides, ignoring the puddles on the street and the people standing around them. This same soon halted, turned to his friends, and asked whether the sight of all those unguarded cars on an almost-empty street didn't want to make them *kick some scuttlebutt*. He then initiated on his own what was soon to become a group-wide laugh-fest, using words like *light draught, headway, pilot boat, cuntline* and *cox-swain*—"Pitchpole the pilot boat!"—he recalled a certain shared history, a situation analogous to today's, and the adventure or misadventure they'd experienced on that occasion.

With the exception of Ti-Jus, whose hilarity remained subdued, the other slangsters burst into as loud a laughter as they could produce, with the quixotic intention of making themselves heard even beyond the Paris beltway, if not across the Atlantic. To fuel his friends' mirth, or to sustain his own, the hulk with the comb kept repeating "*pilot boat*," dragging out the *i* and then protruding his jaw to form a foghorn *o* that dissolved into a deep rumble. He accompanied his words with hand gestures, though the movements he performed had nothing to do with the things being said. He approached a car, attempted to force open the front door, then the back—in vain. He griped, his voice betraying some annoyance while preserving the still fresh and vibrant imprint of their laughter:

"What's with this Ro-Ro!"

Besides causing neighboring pigeons and sparrows to take flight and bystanding humans to jump, the loud smack the hulk gave to the roof of the locked sedan roused his whistling friend, who came to a stop in front of a curbside mailbox and struck up his own percussion solo on its metal plating. Brows creased, as if in pain, lips and eyes closed, in thrall to some passion, he seemed carried away by his groove, ready to drum for hours under the falling rain; but he just as suddenly abandoned his bongo, eyes now darting around in all directions, searching hyperactively for some specific thing: nothing here, nothing over there either . . . But he finally spotted it, in the transparency of a nearby phone booth: an abandoned newspaper. He wanted to set it on fire, to make it a torch, which he would then slip flaming into the mailbox. It was raining too hard, however. The fire took at first but went out before the drummer could pass it through the slot; then it lit again, but barely, and finally wouldn't light at all. Furious, the failed arsonist yelled that this thing *unhooked his slings*, and he swore at the newspaper, at the cigarette lighter, at the celestial downpour—"Fucking rain!"

While this was going on, Ti-Jus was ambling distractedly down the middle of the street—where the ascetic smoker was shuttling urgently back and forth in increasingly nervous switchback movements. One boy's gait was smooth and supple, while the other's steps fell roughly on the blacktop. Or, again: one's sneakers grazed the puddles carelessly, while the other purposely dredged his thick soles through the water . . . Whatever the case, between the four of them, the young people took up enough space in the street that no passerby could escape their omnipresence—especially since, whether five meters away or fifty, they called to one another incessantly, at the top of their lungs, gesticulating broadly, or, as a threesome, called upon themselves to witness what the fourth was up to—keying a series of parked cars, uprooting a signpost and throwing it to the ground—all displaying an equal capacity to make even the most tenuous gesture into an offensive act, and to turn the slightest statement into a tirade.

Faced with such a commotion, such energy, people turned their distraught gazes toward the phone booth, the entrances to buildings, the windows lighting up the façades, tormented with regret, regret that they themselves weren't safe behind some wall or else at the other end of a phone call. Here was someone leaning forward and stretching his neck as though in full flight but powerless to take the first step. Here was someone else who'd embarked upon his getaway only to renounce it the next instant, defeated at the mere sight of a keypad door lock. Likewise, when one of the boys was heading straight for a lady with an umbrella, she yearned to step to one side, but could not. Hardly had she moved her foot, hardly had she turned her body off course, than—as efficiently as though it were being guided by a mooring rope—the muddle of her mind returned it back to its original position; and since he hadn't deviated from his path either, the boy was soon upon her: would she mind if . . . ? The smoker or the hulk with the comb, he hunched his back, scrunched his head between his shoulders and flexed his knees: the taller of the two trying to make himself smaller, the wetter of the two trying to slip under the umbrella, next to the lady as yet untouched by the rain. Nasty weather, isn't it . . . ? What was her name? Did she live nearby? Did she like younger men . . . ?

"Here, I'll give you a hand," addressing her familiarly all of a sudden, while at the same time grabbing the umbrella's handle.

He then called the others over.

"Hey, Teej! Yo, Whistler! Over here, we're all gonna get friendly!"

Ti-Jus responded by sizing the lady up; The Whistler with a jibe:

"Don't forget to heave the fothering, you jerk!"

Then he pounced on another umbrella. He asked the young couple sheltering underneath for a cigarette; from the girl in particular, he asked about the gold bracelet she wore on her wrist, and wondered whether she would agree to *swab the decks* or *buck up the baguette* on a handsome young man like him. He persisted. It would be awfully nice . . . All right, too bad—but the boyfriend would do in a pinch, *buck up, swab,* wouldn't he . . . ? He was right up in the boyfriend's face, after closing in on the girl, and his right hand stayed inside his jacket pocket, as if in readiness, maybe for real this time, to pull a knife on them.

The young couple was rescued by a warning from the hulk with the comb, one that applied to everyone: have to be careful; if Ti-Jus gets into the act, things could get ugly . . . The friend under the umbrella shouted his opinion on the matter for all to hear, though with minimal articulation and a sluggish delivery better suited to soliloquy. He recoiled then, turned his face away, closed his eyes—but recoiled, turned, and closed only halfway, so that these hints of vague and perhaps feigned anxiety were only partly converted into a look of rapture. For his part, easily impressed, and lending to his effusions the same greedy nuance as someone else's "What a schmuck!" or "No way!," the ascetic smoker appealed then to the *hawseholes*, in his slang, and likewise to all kinds of *fairleads*: *winch, hawse, roller fairleads, Panama fairleads*. Or he wagged his head, at a loss for words entirely.

Every man and woman in the street felt that his or her free will had been repossessed and was now concentrated entirely in the person of Ti-Jus; and now all these people, the street, all things looked on as Ti-Jus performed. He had done nothing thus far except pick up the deracinated pole left on the sidewalk; but the sign's aggressively scarlet color, as well as the young man's visibly determined expression and long nervous fingers—gripping their prize like the pole of a halberd—already bore within them the act about to be committed, and even its outcome: were already actualizing the moment, the flash of contact between safety glass and metal, resulting in an entire side of the phone booth exploding into thousands of shards, partly scattered across the pavement, partly piled on the aluminum floor inside the booth, with still another segment of glass dangling precariously in place, festooning the interior rim of the frame with their pathetic but threatening slivers.

By the time any of the witnesses recovered from the shock, the four boys had decamped, causing an agitation that spread as they progressed.

With quickened breath and voices shaken by the headlong race, they were already recalling the disorderly narrative of what had only just taken place to one another. They laughed themselves into hiccups. And thus, running, all the while laughing, talking, panting, without seeming to realize that anything had changed—that they were moving over a different kind of ground, that they had entered another acoustic atmosphere, a more compact crowd, dryness after the rain—they crossed the threshold of the Gare de Lyon, on the side where trains depart for the suburbs.

2. 06

On the bridge, during watch, provided the weather is fine and no warning lights are on at the control panel, and the radar screen isn't showing any potential obstacles in our path, our thoughts turn purposefully toward places that, though scattered wide across the globe, are, within us, adjacent to one another, and, however dissimilar, embrace us all, simply because we've dwelt—just once, or several times—in each. Thus, as we sail surrounded by nothing but ocean and the encircling horizon, our memory's eye passes earthly sites in review, sites that it beholds in full or examines in detail, as it pleases, moving from cyclone to snowstorm and from springtime to rainy seasons great and small, from the Lombardy poplar planted along new suburban avenues to the casuarinas of upscale housing, to the kola tree, to the banana grove. It lingers at the sight of a street without sidewalks, where makeshift market stalls spill their pungent odors onto the pavement, but also at a view of white highlights imprinted by frost on the stone statuary in public parks. A boulevard where tall new buildings and older ones are juxtaposed, another lined with flamboyants, trunks whitewashed, and houses with corrugated tin roofs—both sparking an identical excitement of recollection. Or even pondering the *Francilien* reality all at once, impossible though it may be to embrace both Bagneux and Fresnes, Fresnes and Ris-Orangis, or more generally *départements* Nine-One and Seven-Five together, yet the eye of memory can make them one, composing—with what they offer by way of landscape, activity, and assorted extras—a single, inexhaustible image, in which a shift from the tarmac at Orly West to the ballast at the Maisons-Alfort train station can take place with as little a sense of transition as in moving from a downtown Paris street crowd into a group of young people conversing under the blinking neon sign of the Évry Bowling Alley, or from these sights to Celestin in the process of buying loose tobacco at the Le Beuilhet café-tobacconist's in Beuilhet Alley.

Is it because of the time of day? The inclement weather? The season? Or has it always been thus, here on solid ground, at least in lands as yet unvisited by Refusal? The atmosphere is ominous in Beuilhet. Talk and gestures here are nothing more than faint-hearted attempts at maintaining a modicum of speech and activity in a café-tobacconist's surrounded within a radius of several dozen kilometers by wasteland, perhaps in ruins, or merely ill-formed, in any case unfit for both factual and verbal fulfillment. The clanking of glass, plastic, or porcelain against stainless steel or laminate is more likely to be heard than the voices of the customers standing at the counter or sitting at tables—than the owner's voice, or the waiter's, the tobacconist's, or that of Celestin, who hasn't uttered a word since he entered, except to say "a pack of" followed by his brand of loose tobacco. Hardly more talkative, the tobacconist merely states the price of the purchase, which she then places in front of her—and in doing so, while she receives her payment, and likewise while Celestin, one-handed, clumsily collects his change, she keeps her eyes riveted to him, as though he is wounded, disfigured, monstrous, or has the absent look of figures in paintings carrying a dead body in their arms, or lifting a heavy decapitated head by the hair, and who, yoked to their load, seem themselves to have already entered the world beyond the grave, such that the living are stunned to discover them still in their midst.

Celestin exits, replaced in the space of the café by an icy draft that the local warmth is quick to absorb. Celestin is back home, the rain falls unabated, the doors of the Opel slam and Bessie arrives in turn, accompanied by Madame Fenerolo.

"Are you home?" she asks, from the entryway.

No answer. Bessie sighs and addresses Celestin a second time, "Are you home?," before announcing "Madame Fenerolo is here for a fitting"; after another pause, another sigh, she says to the manager "That's just the way he is."

The visitor assumes an air signifying "I know, it's alright," or "No problem." Yet in the moments that follow, while letting her gaze wander distractedly over the living room, she addresses Celestin at a distance.

"Hello, Celestin."

She idles, dreamy-eyed, her body generous in its verticality, in its ease of movement within the room's dry, stable atmosphere. She lays her pelisse across the back of the sofa bed. Her shoulder grazes the wooden frame of the swing mirror, as do her fingers the sheer cotton curtains that veil the windows. She looks at the photograph of Ti-Jus set atop the television set, and her hand having reached for the maidenhair fern next to the picture frame, she strokes the underside of the delicate foliage, dilating her nostrils as if to relish the earthy scent of humus . . . Neither of the women, nor Celestin, have said anything during this perusal; and in the absence of human voices, the various rinse, fill, and flush noises coming from the kitchen, or from neighboring units in the building—as well as the air, impalpable, floating through the apartment between floor and ceiling—all assign new meaning to their respective liquid and gaseous states, thereby underscoring the close affinity, as solids, between the objects, plants, and living creatures gathered together at the Deux-Rivières apartment.

Outdoors, things are different. Blurred by the rainy dusk until completely subsumed into the sinister lamplight, creatures and objects have lost all outline, practically all materiality. In such conditions, a walker feels as though he is moving into a landscape without boundaries, toward which fragments of his person rush, pointlessly, alone in the world, while he watches in close-up as they precede his face, subliminal. He is elated, almost delirious—yet steeped in the oppressive sense of existing in a place where none of his fellows exist. Should he discern someone in the distance, however, his attention will be focused entirely upon that image, out there, which imposes a presence as unlike the void as his own: heavy in the air, dense among the mists, impermeable to rain, and isolated within the warmth of its winter clothing.

Yet as soon as the doors to the Opel slammed a moment ago, Ti-Jus and Madame Fenerolo—he having come from the Ris train station and about to arrive at the Mermoz Projects, she with car keys in hand, standing next to her car—were that walker and that far-off presence, respectively. Had the manager remained stationary, the young man would have seen her grow larger bit by bit, finally taking shape. The standard feminine outline of the first instants would have gradually broken up into various zones—head, trunk, limbs—or into even and uneven zones—convex or concave—then neck, face, hair, gloved and ungloved hands, high heels, left and right ankles, as well as the parts of both legs located between pelisse and ankle. Instead of which, having walked briskly around her Opel, Madame Fenerolo disappeared behind Bessie into the entrance to Stairwell H.

2. 07

Tart trace of lemon, cloying sweetness of wild island blackberry, a dull but persistent hint of camphor, the same scents he encountered at the entrance and that accompanied him up the stairwell greet Ti-Jus at home. It's the moment when Celestin drops the glass in the kitchen, or knocks over his stool. Halted on the threshold of the living room, Ti-Jus breathes deeply. He hears the shattering of glass, the stool hitting the floor, and soon his mother's voice—"Everything all right?"—and Madame Fenerolo's—"So?"—and again his mother's voice responding, "It's all right, nothing serious."

When they become aware of a presence in the room, the two women start. Bessie's hand goes to her chest.

"You scared me," she says to her son.

The son replies in a mumble that sounds something like "way down," "A-bomb," "hemlock," or, terribly mangled, a piece of "Hey Mom"; a cursory reply, in any case, rendered all the more so because, instead of shoring it up with a look or gesture, Ti-Jus lets his body continue on its way, while his eyes size up Madame Fenerolo in her wraparound skirt and tight turtleneck sweater.

Later on, the young man moves thoughtlessly around the apartment. Boom box under his arm, music blaring, he crisscrosses the living room where the fitting is taking place, and finally settles right in as spectator.

He pulls over one of the dining-room chairs and straddles it backwards, arms crossed around its back and hand resting atop the crest. Bessie eyes him obliquely, so nearby in his plaster-speckled blue jeans, barefoot, bare-chested, and skin still moist from his recent shower. She turns toward him, on the verge of demanding firmly that he clear out, or at least that he look elsewhere, at least back up a bit, at least turn down the volume . . . But placing her hand on the seamstress's shoulder, Madame Fenerolo signals they would do better to disregard this display of adolescent pigheadedness.

"Ignore him, Bessie. Let's just go on, shall we?"

A pause, as Bessie makes up her mind. Then, finally, won over by the manager, she resumes the fitting, but not without wagging her head in dismay at her son's provocation, causing the tape measure around her neck to oscillate wildly. She checks to see that the chest darts and shoulder pads of the new jacket are all in place. She removes a stray thread, a hair clinging to the anthracite-black serge. She squats, or kneels, and from the velvet pin cushion attached to her left forearm, she extracts one, then two pins, and so on, expertly sticking each into the hemline of a pant leg.

On the rug where she stands equidistant from the swing mirror, the TV set, and the sofa bed, Madame Fenerolo hardly budges, though she moves just enough that the ceiling behind her supposedly motionless hair appears to be swaying. The elapsing seconds or minutes are moments of stillness: long, steady minutes of calm. On his own initiative, out of dislike for the song just announced or else an urge for silence, Ti-Jus switches off his radio; or if it's still on, for whatever reason, the sound is now so low as to evoke a boat at anchor, by the motionless shore, while we, coming off the boat, have set foot upon land, the rarefied noises of life onboard reaching us now only after the fact—the ship's cook among his pots and pans, a sailor scraping rust or hammering a machine part—sounds that die away in the air: so infinitesimal between the surface of the water and the canopy of heaven that we're made to feel—along with the sheer size of the universe—a mournful astonishment at no longer rolling with the waves or gripping a rail.

"Here's what it looks like," says Bessie, pairing a rotation of her torso toward the mirror with a withdrawal of her body from her subject.

In turn, Madame Fenerolo turns toward the mirror where she is faced with the results of the pinning process. She sees an improvement—"Yes, that's much better . . . yes, I like it better that way." Yet Bessie is concerned: don't the hips need letting out after this adjustment? Isn't the crotch a little too tight . . . ? She says *hips* and *need letting out*, but not *crotch*, for which she substitutes an indicative chin movement, a look, a raised eyebrow and the word *here*, as in: "Doesn't it feel too snug here?," or "Isn't it a bit too tight here?"

The two women talk leg turn-up and sleeve length, thread color and buttons. One busying herself, the other holding her pose, they wonder what should be worn with a suit like this. A blouse? What color, what fabric . . . ? As for shoes, they should be refined, black, or a nice gray; high heels, of course—gray crocodile, something in gray crocodile would look good, what does Bessie think?

Questions such as this one, of the "seafood counter" type, act upon the organism with violence. The unease we experience at first soon worsens, grows oppressive. Icy currents course through the abdominal cavity; the pharynx and larynx contract, the stomach turns; finally, with all functions disrupted, our bodily fluids flow to the coarse, shivering surface of our skin, our flesh itself on the verge of spilling out of our mouth. Hence, our failing consciousness barely distinguishes outside from inside. It conjoins them, as does our eye to sea and sky on the far horizon, or the elongated pattern of cirrus clouds and the shoreline; or, again, as when, deep within us, we're unable to distinguish between desire and rage, resentment and remorse, while we're most ravaged by emotion. Likewise, ever since "What do you think, Bessie?," this Indistinctiveness has advanced to the point where the room no longer contains a single physical being nor even an ideal object whose identity has not been significantly diminished: the mirror is hardly more mirror than television, than sofa, the women hardly more women than mere reflections of women, or worse, neither is more noticeably Deux-Rivières than Fenerolo, nor is rebellion still distinct from submission.

Meanwhile, unharmed by the prevailing transformation, Ti-Jus nevertheless entertains no thoughts of flight, nor of attempting to save himself from it. He remains seated, legs stretched out on either side of the chair back on which his arms rest, lazily. . . He's enjoying this brush with danger, in fact—and the chance to see the manager up close, to breathe in the scent of camphor trees freely . . . He even slang-talks to himself, agitated beneath his languid exterior and further aggravating his state by crudely designating its causes as "Fucking stern rope!" and "Clinometer's going fucking crazy!" and "VHF 16!" He says to himself, "I'll get there, someday I'll get there." Such sensual expectations! Rock-solid ground underfoot; to walk upon, or run, or to take one's rest; the eye embraces many a place down below, many a place displaying its slopes and shadows, its crests, its sun-drenched valleys, exuding its earthly scents, the sound of its flora rustling intermittently, its brooks babbling.

Against all this, Refusal is powerless.

2. 08

With signs and wonders, with overwhelming force, and in next to no time, they would have had to engulf everything. Failing this, to destroy: massively, coldly, patiently, to destroy. Uproot tree and grass, tear out pipes and wiring, shatter the mirror, scatter the echoes. Then destroy some more. Walls, partitions, ceilings, even rock and earth—smash them, cleave them, sow salt into the soil. And still more destruction. Level the mountains: add wreckage to the wreckage, mix ashes into to the slime until the riverbeds were level with the riverbanks, until nothing remained of Île-de-France but endless flats, no shadows being cast save the lone shadow of Refusal.

At such a price, yes, perhaps the *Franciliens* might have been able to recollect the hemispheric abyss always over their heads, toward which—spontaneously—the body rises up, towards which it turns its face; looking out at the stark horizon, watchful, they might have been able to imagine themselves far away, elsewhere; as they advanced, they would have felt that the entire planet in its pliable vastness was carrying them along, urging them on. But—this engulfing and leveling not having come to pass—people were seized by bewilderment instead. They ran. Darting about aimlessly, wincing, eyes turned heavenward and mouths open to the wind, they trampled the suburban esplanades and shook the black-topped metal of the pedestrian overpasses spanning the rush of traffic on the avenues below. They smashed into walls, into rough cinderblock and concrete pillars. They collapsed, or hovered in sorrow and disgust over those who had collapsed. They dug themselves into vegetable gardens, between plastic sheets and wooden planks, or behind the inept shelter of an old car up on cinderblocks in some graveled backyard. Or again, heavy with fatigue and shame, they staggered across uneven embankments, surrounded by the scattered silhouettes of apartment blocks in the distance, defoliated woodlands, construction cranes, or the outlines of office buildings secluded amid plowed fields or gaps in the highway system—where one might have thought all reality had been pushed back, to the limits of the visible, beyond reach of the runaways, condemned therefore to wander eternally.

They lacked the strength to go on. They soon quit running, hiding. Gradually, the din of the present yielded to a silence in which some terrible future was surely building momentum. A last engine shut off. A last crow cawed between Fresnes Prison and Thiais Cemetery. A last car radio fell silent. Then the *Francilien* voices commenced their lament: so depleted, so disunited, that at first, one would have thought the sounds had emerged from beneath the earth itself; then, however, joined together, a huge, gasping pneumatic mass, it contorted over the surface of the entire region, conforming to the natural relief of the landscape, or even adding new features—here the dolorous swelling of a chorus, there the collapse of a solo reduced to a long sigh. And everywhere, finally, the hands, the *Francilien* hands that gestures of despair had thus far kept closed in on themselves or pressed against the chest or forehead, these hands, laboriously unfolding their prehensile fingers, rose now above heads, or else, forsaken, waved about in the void; these hands exposed their palms, their soft undersides, so uncannily pale—more vulnerable even than a throat offered up to the switchblade's edge, than the eye to a burning fire, than the belly to the beaks, claws, and fangs of earthly predators.

Far from this mournful scene, however, Ti-Jus and the girl in the blue sweater were holding one another in a tight embrace, finding in their shared slang a suitable accompaniment to their tryst, when indeed they said anything at all. They did make a promise to *unreeve*, to *ease off the main*, until the *anchor's aweigh* was pronounced. They kept their word and during the maneuver said "heave to," "slow as she goes," or "full speed ahead," accentuating the smooth stillness of the space around them with their noises, or else, at intervals, setting off a new onslaught—an uproar, even—in that same space, its silence bearing down on them. After which, she or he whispered "They'll be back any minute . . . we have to get out of here," though neither made a move to rise. With the tips of her fingers, the girl cleared a wisp of hair from her own face, a little sweat from the boy's. They kept repeating "We have to clear out of here," and finally did get up, because the regular occupants of the residence were in fact liable to arrive at any moment.

Considering where she was and how little dressed, the girl with the blue sweater was behaving nonetheless as though she were at home and, at the very least, wearing panties. Moving about quite naturally, crouching down and getting back up, not the least bit shy, she collected her clothes and undergarments, tossed around the room, before bringing Ti-Jus his belongings. She handed him each article one by one, offsetting this solemnity with a touch of abruptness—"Here's your underwear," "Here are your blue jeans" . . . On occasion, having started extending her hand toward the young man with this or that item of clothing, she would pull it back at the last moment to cuddle it between shoulder and cheek; then, with a sudden brutality, would bite down on it. She would laugh, and just as suddenly recover her seriousness.

"Here's your T-shirt."

Ti-Jus took the T-shirt, put his underwear back on, slipped into his jeans. He'd just passed the palm of his hand and five fingers over his face: one time, with care, from the upper forehead to the chin, as much to hasten the progress of the stream of water he'd just splashed on himself as to lower the curtain—so to speak—on what had just transpired. So that now, refreshed and closely-shaven, he has finished getting dressed; but it's another day—closer than yesterday to what's about to happen—and he's in another apartment, whose doorbell the hulk with the comb is about to ring.

2. 09

Celestin came out of the kitchen for the occasion and gazed upon his son, his wife, and the package she was holding at a careful horizontal angle before entrusting it to the youth. The friend with the comb was there as well. Wearing his tight-fitting bomber jacket, clunky work boots, and a skull-hugging knit cap, he clashed with his living-room surroundings no less than did Ti-Jus, with his heavy pullover and motorcycle jacket—too big, too voluminous for the size of the room, and incongruously overdressed in his winter apparel, given the effectiveness of the floor-to-ceiling heating system. There was still some daylight outdoors: not for much longer, but it was still light. The visible presence of the space outdoors—so vast, and starting so abruptly just beyond the plate glass—was constantly prompting heads to pivot toward the windows. Bessie, like Celestin, yielded to this tropism; and even Ti-Jus, when he gives the signal for departure, will address his "Let's go!" less to his friend than to the wide, glittering world for which they are about to depart.

Ever since the package had changed hands, Bessie kept her arms folded over her chest, not knowing what to do with her hands, with her fingers, not knowing where or how to stand in the room. She asked two, three questions that met with silence, resigned from the outset to her queries going unanswered: did Ti-Jus know how to get there . . . ? shouldn't he wear a scarf . . . ? a knit cap . . . ? She had time enough to sigh, to look out the window, to sigh once more, and then, having spotted a thread coiled around the kraft paper, to step over to her ruby, azure, and lemon-yellow boy before proffering her final piece of advice: don't spoil anything. She bowed her head, or inclined it to one side, as if her neck had weakened beneath the weight of foreboding. The smell of dinners on stoves was rising up the stairwell, to which a gust of wind, suddenly rattling the door hinges, added a fleeting note of wintry air. A neighbor was sawing boards, drilling holes. The high-pitched buzz of the electric drill or the scraping of the handsaw intermittently drowned out the distant sound of both television sets and their spectators. Footsteps and voices would soon be heard as well, converging on a table where something like a steaming soup pot would be placed; a hammer would be heard pounding plastic dowels into freshly drilled holes; on countless screens, the same armed militia would be walking through the same wreckage, the same dapper old gent at the wheel of the same roadster would be heading for the same border—he would stop at a gas station, have some coffee at the counter of an adjoining diner, stare for a while at a girl, almost a child, dancing to the sounds of an old jukebox. And the more the sounds and smells heralded actions and situations such as these, the more it became obvious that the two boys would not be partaking in any of them, nor would they even bear witness thereof. On every floor of every stairwell in the Mermoz Projects, people sitting down to dinner would be drinking, eating; meanwhile, the boys would be heading toward the ground floor, flying down the stairs. One by one, the hooks, catches, or struts would be screwed into the walls; the boys would feel a sudden rush of cold air prick their faces and hands. On the screens, an officer in uniform standing at the threshold of the diner would see the dapper old gent near the jukebox; the boys would be walking around a parked car, winding their way between two others, crossing Beuilhet Alley, to move off, solitary, across the muddy vacant strip that separated them from Avenue de Paris, heading straight for Vallon.

When the time actually comes for them to be eclipsed into the distance, the vacuum created back at the Deux-Rivières apartment by the boys' departure is still so tangible that both Bessie and Celestin have trouble getting their bearings, startled when their gazes fail to collide with the massive presence of the hulk with the comb, or the lithe verticality of Ti-Jus. They are on familiar, home terrain, but move around clumsily, stand in place awkwardly. Celestin periodically comes to a sudden stop in his meandering around the living room, awaiting who knows what; or he starts walking sideways, limping as though avoiding some obstacle on the mosaic flooring. It takes Bessie's voice announcing that she's going to make dinner, or informing him of what menu she has in mind, for the domestic space to recover its wholeness, for it to become a pliable medium once again, open to the steady course of sound and silence, and in which nothing—not even a slight turbulence, not even the discreet stippling of a seamstress's stitch—remains of what had briefly disturbed it.

Meanwhile, despite the craters, the bumps, and the bits of rusty metal strewn in the mud, Ti-Jus and his sidekick pursue their rectilinear path. The crumpling and occasional cracking of their leather jackets penetrated by the northerly winter wind as it whistles around their ears, as well as the endless rumble of traffic on the Avenue de Paris, have gradually eliminated the sounds of the Mermoz Projects, which, after having first been the place they'd broken away from, then the place they'd left behind, has now joined the land of Elsewhere—a space where compass points dance in constant and capricious flux.

Ti-Jus takes the lead, mute, his face expressionless, his extended forearms perfectly parallel to the ground as they bear the package to be delivered. Though trying his best to emulate this sober demeanor, the hulk with the comb can't help but chatter, even if reduced to monologue, or to kid around, even if he laughs alone. Jokingly, though proud of his new look, he removes his knit cap to reveal a shiny, shaven skull.

"You see this?" he shouts into the wind.

He's shaken by silent laughter that causes him to lower his eyelids and sets him to nodding. Later on, the bald head now recapped, he swears under his breath: "Bitchin'!" or maybe "Itchin'!" or "Avast this bullshit." Still later, out of nowhere, he asks Ti-Jus what he's got in the package—"What's that you got in the package?"

Ti-Jus is tight-lipped.

The friend goes "Huh?" by way of a second attempt, raising his voice, thinking he had not been heard. In a third attempt, removing 's that and in the package, he goes "Whatchou got?" before finally offering an answer to his own question—a general term such as clothes, or perhaps threads, "I'll bet it's threads," or some other slang expression.

The vacant strip and empty sky recede before the boys' advance, recede all the way to the guardrail that lines the Avenue de Paris. Visible above the rail, the car roofs scintillate in an unlikely shimmering of heat, giving off inscrutable signals that could belong just as well to the gray, pale yellow, and mauve mass of clouds above them as to the grayish beige ground below. Every so often, against a background of noise that distance deadens and disassociates from the visible, a puddle laps at one of their shoes, or the kraft paper quivers, giving a dry rustle in the wind. On the horizon, to the left, tall apartment towers are silhouetted in miniature. The hulk with the comb points in their direction.

"That's Évry over there," he asserts, though his voice betrays uncertainty, even a pronounced drift toward the interrogative.

He's slowed down, eyes still on the towers, as one does when the fleeting sight of something enjoyable makes one want to prolong the vision, or when the tedium of daily life manages to confer some entertainment value on even the simplest occurrence. He soon finds he has to hurry, almost run to make up the lost distance between him and Ti-Jus. His foot slips. He swears, "itchin'!," once again, or "three shits to the wind!'" Then, having managed to recover, he gradually catches his breath. In his field of vision, the continuity of the crosscutting guardrail in the distance is broken up only by the Ti-Jus's back in the foreground—rising, falling, rising, falling in a steady, alternating movement—together with the two sagging extremities of the package showing beyond the shoulder guards of the boy's leather jacket. A long moment elapses, with neither boy uttering a word. The first is unshakeable in his ceremonious procession, driven by some inner purpose—to levitate, to personify at one and the same time the arrow and the arrow's trajectory, its target and its arc, or else to condense within himself, as he marches toward Vallon, the entirety of his own story, from *Radio messages* to *plasmaphele*. The face and movements of his friend, however, reveal on the contrary the unstable disposition of someone constantly barraged by inchoate ideas, images, fleeting memories, or snatches of speech. Simultaneously *betwixt* and *ballast* pop into his mind, one seeking solitude, lingering as though weightless beneath his knit cap, the other gregarious but soon dissipating, having been unable to cull the other words that together might have formed a complete sentence. Voice regained at last, the hulk again raises his head and stretches his neck to hail Ti-Jus:

"No clue?" . . .

He calls to mind a certain country he's heard of. He neither names nor situates it, but in a gesture that enthusiasm would further expand, were it not curbed by regret, he implies that it is a faraway, if not wholly inaccessible land.

An explanation follows, in the course of which the word *girls* returns insistently, as does the snapping of fingers. "All you have to do is," he says—his middle finger snaps. He continues with "All of them, if you want," and swears to Ti-Jus that it really does work like that, over there.

"Can you imagine!"

He, for one, can imagine. He eyes the terrain on all sides, as if there were girls to be had in droves right there on the vacant strip, all obligingly complacent, the wind teasing their garments, their gazes feverishly indiscreet, light and lithe, airborne, needing nothing more to propel their approach, withdrawal, or return than the smallest undulation of a hip or quivering of a lock of hair.

After that, since in actual fact there are no girls to be seen on that vacant strip of land, the friend feels time is dragging. He looks backward, over his shoulder, or forward, over Ti-Jus's, trying to estimate how far they've come, and how far they still have to go. From the color of the sky, he locates the east and the west, and then an approximate south, whence countless migrating birds fly back up to Île-de-France every spring. He spits, lights a cigarette, talks to Ti-Jus—does he know, with regard to birds, which kind of seagull is also called a *senator*? What kind of lifeboat a *seagull* is? That *turkeys* used to be called *guinea fowl*? That—speaking of "used to"—*companion* used to mean eating the same bread?

2. 10

"*Com-pain*," says the companion. "*Companion* used to be *com-pain*. Before."

And then, as though there were some connection:

"So what's she like, the client?"

The monologue stops there, leaving the walkers' silence to rub grimly against the silence of the deserted strip. Time passes uneventfully, marked only by the repetition of footsteps that fall as though by routine, outside any prospect of arrival and beyond the memory of any departure. Hence the need for the hulk with the comb to search elsewhere for material to revive their conversation.

"Over at The Whistler's place," he begins.

He continues, situating the setting of his anecdote with more precision—"the old market gardeners' place"—and then providing a vague time reference—"the other day." He talks about the eleven-year-old kids, or not even eleven, that hang out in gangs; about cats being stoned to death—and not only stoned, and not only cats.

"You should have seen 'em *hawsehole* it!"

Silence. Then "I'm not shitting you," "I swear," or "Swear." Then more silence, before a final word on the subject suggests that this closing remark is the end product of a laborious mulling over of the available material.

Then, after crossing some intangible but decisive line, the noisy proximity of traffic suddenly relegates the silent flatness of the vacant strip to the background. No more mulling over, no more talk of stoning nor any other event unrelated to the here and now—henceforth the future looms, and the only actions that matter are those that will hasten its unfolding: walking, moving forward, right up to the guardrail, climbing over it, and then, having climbed over it, crossing the road while looking straight ahead, paying no heed to oncoming traffic.

Over at Vallon, meanwhile, at the entrance to the apartment complex of the same name, three young girls unanimously suspend their gossiping to raise their eyes toward Avenue de Paris. They have heard the sudden screeching of tires on the asphalt, followed by the furious volleys of car horns and shouts. Wincing, they dip their heads between their shoulders as arms straighten at their sides, or fists nestle against their sternums.

When, at the embankment's crest, haloed in a mix of fog, prematurely lit streetlamps, and waning daylight, Ti-Jus and the hulk with the comb appear, the girls immediately alter their attitudes. The first affects cool composure, nonchalance, tries to look adult. The other two, on the contrary, display their excitement by exclaiming *did you see that* and *they must be out of their minds.*

"Out of their minds!" repeats one of the girls, making room between *out of their* and *minds* for the full quantity of their stifled disbelief.

Then, with surprise, voice raised an octave and finger pointed toward the boys:

"Wait, I know who they are!"

At this, the two excited girls' eyes meet, resulting in a burst of hysterical laughter—who knows why . . . ? Whatever the reason, they're doubled over, mouths producing a convulsive cloud of blue steam, cheeks aflame, braided hair jolting against their temples in beaded bunches . . . and every time they're about to settle back down, the littlest thing—a look, a wink or the merest vocalization—sets them off again.

As for the nonchalant third girl, entirely unaffected by her friends' hilarity, at most displaying an indulgent smile, she moves a few steps away, as if absentmindedly, to position herself dead-center between the two pillars flanking the apartment-building entrance. She is humming a tune, but so low as to be practically inaudible; or without actually humming, she makes a point of keeping her lips parted, while swiveling her upper body on her childlike pelvis, rocking mischievously. What will happen when, with their height, their build, and their long stride, the boys come face to face with her? As tall as they are, will they even notice her presence? Muscular and well built as they appear to her, will they be capable of stopping the momentum of their own mass . . . ? Will the first one jostle her? Will the second, without interrupting his forward motion, grab her by the shoulders and lift her off the ground . . . ?

The laughers have stopped laughing, amazed by what's happening, full of curiosity about what's to come. With lowered voices, they exchange forecasts.

"They'll walk around her."

"She'll move out of the way."

The nonchalant girl *does* move out of the way—or, in any case, at the last minute, in order to avoid any possibility of being grabbed, lifted, or jostled, she whirls around, and at the same time enunciates, offhandedly, "You coming, girls?"

On the private grounds of the Vallon Apartments, at the hour when all the outdoor lighting blinks on, three small persons move forward, like an escort, ahead of the two older boys. By turn, each of the three young girls improvises some special mode of progressing along the procession route—one starts running, skipping, and after getting ahead, waits or retraces her steps—as if, before the new arrivals, each is anxious to demonstrate her agility and to prove what an advantage it is, in the cramped confines of the apartment complex, to inhabit a body of such minuscule dimensions; unless it's simply an excuse to move against the current, if only for a few seconds, and to get a better look at the two boys, a chance to marvel at the close-fitting knit cap and clunky work boots, and then, face-to-face with the slashed blue jeans, the wooly hair, the sneakers, and

Ti-Jus in the flesh—between sneakers and wooly hair—to develop an instant crush on him.

The security guard isn't on the scene as quickly this time—absent? busy? less zealous . . . ? In the sky above the apartment complex, a clearing between two cloud masses reveals a star—matched, back on earth, though not quite so brilliant in the late afternoon half-light, by the headlights of a car creeping toward the complex's exit. As it passes them, the girls purposely allow the car to brush them, and even lay their hands on it as they murmur some swearword—"Bitch!"—or some demand—"Power to the Pedestrians!" Then, as their target drives away, they burst out laughing; and huddling together as if in some feverish covey, they glorify their respective exploits, inflating that murmur into a shout, transforming the hand into a claw, a fist, and the harmless gesture into a scratch or a smack . . . But whether we're speaking of what they say happened, or of what actually did happen, it was in either case never anything more than a childish trifle; and consequently, nothing that would fail to confer a certain lightness on this unfolding episode, as does the persistent greenery of the privet shrubs or the young pine trees planted here and there around the lawn—or at least to frame the arrival of Ti-Jus and the hulk with the comb as a harmless event, of the sort that neither disturbs the peace of any particular moment nor disrupts the order of the places they occur in. Yet, as the color slowly drains from the sky, dusk itself becomes more severe with each passing moment. One might think it was being haunted by some lethal secret—a day with no promise of a new dawn, an arrival with no assurance of a fresh departure. Or perhaps it's only grieved that the two boys, along with itself, are now captives of the narrow, grassy confines of the apartment complex, when it would so much rather they were all together again in the wide-open spaces of the vacant strip, where only moments before the wind had whistled and whisked away the hulk's dream country, his *gulls*, his "scuttle it" . . . But for whatever reason—dread, affliction, or other—it flinched, the dusk flinched, deploying with great difficulty, by way of its final moments of luminosity, the shadowy fabric of remembrance—not so long ago, remember, the visible world stretched out flat and unending all around us; we gazed upon it with the private gratification of living out of place, out of time—the entire suburb and the delivery boy already cloaked in the old, enduring sadness of "nevermore."

2.11

Nightfall now complete on the other side of the picture windows, the darkness kept the outside world at bay, obscuring the spaces between the zones of light, deepening the sounds engulfed in silence, and estranging all realities—and the very notion of reality. Of course, the long fluorescent stream that cut through the landscape was recognizable as Avenue de Paris, as the red points of light in the distant sky were identifiable as the aerial beacons at Évry, or indeed the dark patch stretching out toward the west as the Bas-de-Ris Woods. But those places pertained to a continuum wholly separate from the manager's apartment. They formed a kind of two-dimensional stage set the eye could scan without penetrating, where imagination met with no boundary. But the apartment, a sculpture in the round, was a space where one might actually move and take definitive action.

As demonstrated daily by Madame Fenerolo. And, in her company, demonstrated that evening by Ti-Jus and the hulk with the comb.

"Come in, come in," said the manager, in the process of removing her gardening gloves.

Then, seeing the package, feigning to have only just noticed it.

"Ah, wonderful!"

She showed the young visitors into the living room, smiling, lively— would they have something to drink—affable in her straight skirt and beneath her V-neck sweater—"Have a seat"—exuding a pleasant camphor-wood scent and, by virtue of her movement about the room, causing another smell to waft through the apartment as well, that of freshly turned potter's soil. The boys said, "Not thirsty, thanks," or "Not thirsty," or a curt "Thanks," with a hand gesture. The friend sat down, Ti-Jus did not. Outdoors, a car was maneuvering between the two buildings of the apartment complex in first gear, its tires on the asphalt making a continuous unsticking noise, a mellow lapping, periodically swelling to more of a short, low sucking sound. Meanwhile, as if they had wandered off into other rooms, or had needed this lapse of time to acclimatize and recover their pungency, the scents ushered in by Ti-Jus and the hulk with the comb had begun to circulate through the living room, adding to the local bouquet hints of fresh air inflected by clay, cold rust, and exhaust fumes. Was Madame Fenerolo vexed by the intrusion of these exogenous odors into her home . . . ? Or, rather, had the manager reacted to the overwhelmingly conspicuous fact of Ti-Jus and his slashed blue jeans . . . ? She was smiling less broadly, had grown nervous, saying one thing, then changing her mind. She had even tripped, and while saying "Ouch! . . . No, it's all right," in order to check one of her high heels, she had brought her foot up to one of her buttocks, and in a single, supple twist, turned her head all the way around, before straightening once again to her initial position. Then, during the opening of the package, with each little fricative produced by the tearing away of the adhesive tape, she had displayed a self-protective reflex motion, rushing with one hand to cover some portion of her skirt, and with the other a bit of her V-neck, and likewise, with the subsequent crumpling of kraft paper, she had stiffened in a brief, tetanic spasm.

The smell of new fabric and thread momentarily superseded the previous odors. Silence weighed heavily before Ti-Jus finally decided to break it.

"You have to try them on."

He was lying.

"My mother wants you to try them on."

With the pants, jacket, and wraparound skirt draped over her fore-arms, Madame Fenerolo had hardly opened the glass-paned door that led down the hall than she paused, fear-stricken, one might have thought, and was tempted to drop the clothing, even to turn left toward the entrance instead of turning right into the bedroom . . . Perhaps, at that instant, the desire to be somewhere else had flashed images of escape through her mind, images of her opening, then carefully closing the door to the landing, descending the five floors by elevator—"Faster! Faster!"—press-ing—"Almost there!"—the DOOR button at the building's exit . . . Alas! faced with the sudden otherness of outside space, she found herself inca-pable of going any further. She called for help, but her voice disappeared into the night. She stretched herself forward into the becalmed empti-ness, making broad distress signals with her arms, but her gesticulations had no audience aside from the three young girls who, either mistaking or mocking, responded from afar by waving their hands gleefully—"*Bon-soir, Bonsoir!*"—before turning away from her.

Yet, acquiescing to her initial intention, Madame Fenerolo had soon disappeared through the glass-paned door to the right, leaving the living room, with all it contained by way of odors, inhabitants, and furniture, al-most in expectation of the events to come. Deeply ensconced in his chair, one hand plastered to his skull and his face wavering between brutality and derision, the hulk with the comb maintained the same silent inertia as the surrounding air, the freshly repotted ficus tree, or the discarded wrapping paper on the living-room table. Ti-Jus was also waiting. He had not stirred from his place, nor changed posture, and, staring into space, he whistled, or at least having moved his lips into a whistling position, he blew, causing his cheeks to palpitate, though without emitting a single note. The only sounds came from the bedroom: an indecipherable rus-tling; while outdoors, every so often, the ghostly voices of the three girls taunting the security guard, and the latter's recriminations, rose up. A final protest resounded, followed by a vague slamming noise—was it a door or shutters? and had the security guard, appearing briefly, beat a hasty retreat . . . ? There was nothing but the silence of anticipation, of the darkness on the other side of the plate-glass windows: the suburban hum as background to the night. A dog barked. After which everything fell silent once again, until down below, emboldened by the blackness of nightfall, one of the girls assaulted the building's façade with shouts of "Hey up there!," prolonging the *hey* so that the call might more surely reach its intended receiver.

Back in the manager's apartment, Ti-Jus was now in a narrow hallway papered with a hummingbird print. He moved forward toward the bedroom, swinging his torso to an inaudible beat accentuated with each step by a bending of his knees, as though, even in the absence of his Walkman, some lively music lodged deep in his ear were keeping him secret company. He was relaxed; and even after he had entered the bedroom, lips still rounded into a whistle, eyes still glazed, he continued his swaying.

The friend listened. Perturbed by yet another "Hey up there," shouted from down below, he showed his annoyance with one of those shakes of the head, those swipes of the hand used in the bush to shoo away mosquitoes. Then, having entered the hallway, and now leaning up against the hummingbird wallpaper, he stayed awhile, nose in the air, mouth open, and brow furrowed with the effort of concentrating . . . At first there was nothing to hear—at least nothing distinct enough to set off his imagination or stimulate an idea. Then, frowning, he turned his head and shot a look in the direction of the manager's bedroom—one that combined frustration, obtuseness, and nascent anger. But then, again, when certain sounds finally became noticeable—the sounds of fabric, of breathing, or of flesh—certain undeniably indecent sounds, that is, his face lit up in a broad, gummy grin; and the indecent sounds now repeating regularly, the hallway was nothing but a succession of pacing and stamping, slapping of the wallpapered walls, of snorts punctuated by fists striking palms and smug snickering: all acts that allowed the previously incredulous friend to confirm with amazement the horizontality of the floor and verticality of the walls, as well as his own capacity for movement within this foreign space.

Yet, all of a sudden, he became sad. He once again leaned up against the hummingbird-patterned wall, arms limp at his sides, heavy giant's hands dangling below, one of them clasping his knit cap with inert fingers that seemed on the verge of letting it drop. Words crossed his mind, like *westerlies*, like *scuttling*, like *embark*, like *take on water*. He greeted each with a cynical mutter, holding them back an instant, then forsaking them altogether. *Westerlies* dropped in silence, tumbling down his sloping body, bouncing off the upper of one of his work boots; and *scuttling* and *embark* and *take on water* all rolled shakily across the carpet in turn, before coming to a stop, joining the ranks of an entire obsolete lexicon, rotting away in oblivion.

Standing up straight again, the friend sighed—for what are words if they are never used . . . ? He scratched his skull, pulled his knit cap back on, sighed anew. Then, after dragging his feet back into the living room, he paused in front of the picture window and gazed out at the nighttime panorama, at the imperfect double exposure of his own reflection onto the nighttime panorama. Finally, strolling around the room, he came upon the mini-fridge at the bar and gave it an apathetic kick, then carelessly overturned a pile of magazines, and even pollarded the ficus tree, before disemboweling a cushion by means of some sharp object found along the way . . . The bottles clinked in the mini-fridge. The magazines spilled onto the floor around the coffee table. The ficus was nothing but the scattered remains of a ficus. As for the cushion, it was now less a cushion than an evisceration, a hole more than anything else, seemingly exposing the rest of the living room to the flow of some unspeakable catastrophe. For the moment, of course, there was nothing but cottony stuffing, whose gradual overspill hardly qualified as a flow at all; but the breach was bound to widen, the tentative stream would become a surge, and once the kapok had poured out, an influx from deep within the inexhaustible elsewhere would follow—from the multiplicity of other apartment spaces and from the stairwell, then from the basement, the plumbing, and the standpipes, then from the suffocating cold of the outdoors and the night, all of which would come and lay siege to the manager's cozy three-room apartment.

This is what the girls down below seemed to be expecting. Standing guard among the parked cars in the visitors' lot, they faced the double-glass doors where the two boys would soon be exiting. Sitting on a car hood, knees curled under her chin and arms hugging her tibias, the non-chalant girl rocked back and forth, looking peaceful and poised in the russet night, level with the other, sparkling vehicles. Her companions, not far off, were standing side by side, the taller tenderly resting her temple on the head of the smaller. At one point, the taller raised her head. The smaller then bent down, immediately swallowed up by her opaque surroundings: hatchbacks, fenders, radiator grills, and metal roofs. Perhaps an itch on her calf, her foot. Or maybe the feeling that one of her socks was twisting around her ankle had begun to annoy her. She had undertaken to scratch the itch, to hike up the sock. But once one or the other gesture had been accomplished, she resurfaced into the car-scape, her lips rounded to produce a huge chewing-gum bubble, making it look as though the girl had bent down in order to grab a toy balloon with her teeth.

3. The Centaur

3. 01

The same relentlessly distressing idea that would by turns propel them headlong or jerk them suddenly to their feet would more often than not sink them back into their seats, or alternatively lay them out flat on the floor, be it parquet or unfinished concrete. This idea armed them with rage, inciting them to knock over plastic trash cans with a vengeance, or else placekick the aluminum cans that littered the street—but it also made them unhappy, abruptly rendering their faces inscrutable, gloomy: burdening their otherwise broad shoulders with invisible entablatures. The idea might occasionally slip their minds, but only the better to settle into their flesh and bite down, enter their arteries and sting; so that, wounded to the quick, the youths would scowl, feral, mumbling or mute, sockets widened in pain and eyes blazing with fury.

Sometimes, shut into a room together, they would look at one another with loathing, curse at each other. It would occasionally end in a fistfight. Face to face, pectoral to pectoral, stomach to stomach, The Smoker and The Whistler would each try to set the other off—"Let's hear that again, punk!" Or the hulk with the comb would give out a brick-breaking karate chop. Or again, Ti-Jus, headphones over his ears, would feign indifference as he fingered the point of his switchblade . . . Their anger would fall away abruptly. There would be silence. If one of them recovered his voice enough to suggest they go out, go over and watch the Seine or have a look around Évry, the answer would invariably be a scornful mumble of sorts.

Fallen silent once again, the four big boys would remain motionless for a time, their arms contorted into various positions, legs spread, crossed, bent at sharp angles, or stretched all the way out. The sum of so many appendages took on colossal proportions, bounded under the same ceiling and within the same four walls, such that it seemed no room could possibly contain a population that size: no living room, not even an entire suburban dwelling, whether it be an apartment or free-standing house.

Outdoors, things were different. There, Ti-Jus and his companions found a space better suited to their dimensions; and though not spared this new space's accompanying burns, bites, or other minor torments, at least they could move about freely, walk, jump, run, break away. And so, they would occasionally be seen in the vicinity of Juvisy, coming from Ris-Orangis by way of Grigny and Viry-Châtillon, walking in single file down the highway. They would be seen at attention at the far end of the landing strips at Orly. They would be seen in Créteil, in Corbeil, in Savigny, slouching across a construction site where, here and there, reddish water stagnated at the bottom of the deep ruts dug out by truck wheels. They strained their voices when they spoke, almost shouting, so that the open sky wouldn't soak up the sound so quickly. They would use words of their own coinage, such as *Furry* and *Reefur, fletch* and *fletching*—"You're fletching my alcides shaft, huh Reefur?" The passing of cars in the other direction wrapped them in a great rush of air. Planes soaring overhead deafened them. The hems of their blue jeans were mud-stained.

But despite the hike and the gusting wind, despite the noise and the mud, despite the new space, the idea remained intact within the boys; and, as before, its persistence would be momentarily betrayed by some reflex movement—one's upper body eager to twist toward nothing, another's eyes darting to turn toward no one . . . And they never failed to spot these signs in each other's behavior, and when they did, their momentum would flag. Except that once in a while, with a burst of energy, a heel would resound more forcefully against the asphalt; or an arm would catapult a stone, aiming for an inaccessible line in the distance defined by a row of poplars, or even beyond the poplars, the two-dimensional profile of a train, or beyond the train, a cluster of miniature buildings that cut a consistent, geometrically vertical silhouette against the horizon.

Sometimes the target was closer at hand, or else the action—whatever it might be—less impossible to accomplish. The result would be several days with glass shards scattered across the sidewalk, at the foot of a large, now exposed municipal bulletin board, or several weeks with a smashed-in bus shelter, or several months' worth of charred phone booth. Discovering this kind of evidence, people knew right away what sort of horde had passed through. They were equally reluctant to linger or to scurry off on their way, tempted by this stroke of luck to venture with impunity into the very place where fate had just struck, but at the same time imagining that lightening could easily strike again, fearing they might suffer the same treatment as the phone booth, the bus shelter, or the municipal bulletin board whose remains were now spread before their eyes.

On the perpetration side, the authors of this mayhem would conduct a four-part recitation of events, with many a repetition and variation— "Remember when we . . . ?" Swearwords and bursts of laughter would be woven into this loose narration. One of the boys would clasp his forehead, face turned skyward in a kind of mystic hilarity. Another would wag his head in disbelief, though thrilled and impressed, repeating, "No way, man!" as he went, stretching out the *way* . . . And then a fresh bite would suddenly interrupt the repartee or the laughter; a new burn would tighten their muscles, causing their bodies to swerve and lurch forward. After which it was once again Grigny, Viry-Châtillon, Juvisy, Corbeil with its old market gardeners' grounds, Créteil and the Baxter Projects. And here or there, either from atop a pedestrian bridge spanning a road, or from down below on an esplanade, the four boys would avidly watch the passing traffic or scrutinize the endless façade of some apartment block, searching outside themselves for the very thing, the idea of which they'd been experiencing inside themselves for so long, anxious to visualize it, at last incarnate, emerging from some automobile or masonry, as in ancient times some ideal creature might have emerged from a tree, the sea, a river, or a rock, come to bequeath upon passersby—be they men or gods—the vision of a tangible beauty.

As it happened, the apparition was greeted with silence—not a move, not a word, four breaths taken away. Then a single, brief, aroused, "Check out the chick!" would unleash other comments, such as an exclamatory "Yeah!" extended over several seconds, or a half-stifled, half-elated "Oh, baby!" or "Fuck," before each retreated once more into silent immutability, all the better to concentrate. Four pairs of eyes would rush to fixate on the same passing crotch. Or alternatively, in a steadier kind of haste, they would scan the remainder of the creature, from top to bottom, as if to better appreciate her simple verticality. And since the girl thus examined was so much a girl, from head to toe, the attraction she exerted would be four-fold, arousing the same violent bondage fantasy in each, the same fantasy of tying up this tangible being, getting her off balance, lifting her up and carrying her off, her body arching helplessly, no part of her touching the ground.

This tangible being, unfortunately, would gradually move away, and finally evaporate. Or else, if the boys had lain in wait for her, in vain, this desertion and absence would now be felt in the landscape as a whole. From here onward, everything there was would be ugly, dismal, despicable: the tar, the clay, the projects, the houses, the market gardens, the fields, the roadways and highways, the roundabouts adorned with flowerbeds, the shopping centers, the playgrounds, the paths worn by the repeated passage of RER rail-commuters. Equally despicable were the scrap iron of automobile graveyards and the plastic of RVs. And again despicable were the cinderblocks, the millstone grit, the concrete or the glass cladding over concrete . . . Wherever there were no girls, what good was all the rest? What did it matter if the day were gloomy or bright? Or whether things existed at all—light, sky, darkness, blue—without girls, what was it worth?

3. 02

Having steered around the paper products display and maneuvered her shopping cart into a new aisle, the shopper was now plowing between two rows of tall shelves stacked with canned goods. Her head was pointed in one direction, her torso and limbs in another, so that the former seemed out of step with the latter. She seemed constantly on the verge of coming to a halt, taking small, indecisive steps as her eyes scanned the upper shelves intently. Further on, in the same aisle, the passage was narrowed considerably by a sizable cardboard box an employee was busy unpacking. The shopper solicited the employee's assistance. Pointing to the item she desired, she asked whether he could help her get it—and he: "That one?" and she: "No . . ." he: "That one?" she: "No, the one next to it, the . . . that's it," then, "Thanks."

This conversation carried over to the adjacent aisle, where, hearing these neighboring voices so distinctly, neither seeing the speakers nor being seen by them, an isolated shopper was struck, intensely, by how opaque the parallel rows on either side of him seemed, and even more intensely by how tall, how perfectly vertical, how narrow, and how oppressively symmetrical they felt. Other sounds also reached his ears, proving that—beyond proximate visibility or invisibility—space did in fact extend beyond the aisle, in all its inhabited diversity. And the promise of this extension, as much perhaps as the nature of the purchases he still had to make, beckoned the shopper toward other areas of the SUMABA.

He entered into the western-most area of the store, where the eye could now circulate unimpeded above the low-mounted freezer compartments, giving the impression that he should also be able to move around the store more freely. Whether this sensation was valid or illusory, in any case the shopper felt suddenly more mobile, more lively, elated by the expansion of his visual field.

Near the entrance, out of the eight checkout lines, which during peak hours would all be working in parallel, only three were open now, and not very busy at that. Directly opposite, behind the glass-encased cheese and deli counter, a twosome in white coats were putting the finishing touches on their daily set-up, the woman fussing with a display of cabécou cheeses, or putting a big chunk of Appenzeller between a Beaufort and a fruity Comté, while the man, reaching his arm over a pan of rillettes, was arranging a garland of Creole-style blood sausages on a circular tray. Over at the meat counter, in a constant shuttling onstage and off, an apprentice butcher was bringing in armfuls of meat. To perform this disappearing/reappearing act, he had to push through a doorway consisting of red and white plastic strips that he would brush aside with either a shoulder or the back of a hand. It looked as though he were cutting his way through a forest, following a path, spying on some intimate scene. Occasionally, having grabbed a handful of strips on his way through, he would slow down as if wanting to prolong the sensation of smooth plastic slipping through his palm and fingers. This annoyed the head butcher who, while continuing to arrange fake foliage and plastic roses around his display, would glare at the apprentice and noisily exhale everything he had been thinking to himself summed up in a *little this* or *little that* and *lazy punk*.

The customers, however, were rapidly growing in number, so that the noises in the store, which at first had resounded distinctly and identifiably beneath its iron girders, were now starting to merge into a general background din. Likewise, the discrete poses and gestures of before had by now fused into one vast swarm, in which the SUMABA brought about a continuous series of transformations, as though this were its natural function: it turned the erratic winds gusting outdoors into a stable indoor atmosphere; the cold into a steady temperature above 72°F; the smell of outdoors—a mix of chlorophyll, blacktop, and car exhaust—into supermarket smell, blending hints of cardboard and detergent with a big bouquet of animal sweat, fruits and vegetables, sawdust; further transformation of merchandise arriving by the pallet, by the gross, by the ton, into purchasable retail units, of car drivers into pedestrians, in turn transformed into action figures pushing, loading, unloading their shopping carts and, once through the checkout line, filling them back up with the same purchases just unloaded.

Bessie, at check-out line 3, would occasionally swivel around to hail some co-worker in deliveries. The rest of the time, she scanned barcode after barcode in a staccato series of beeps, stopping only to ask a shopper to swipe their credit card, or to write out a number herself on the back of a check. Yet, she was under the constant threat of being distracted by notions that would suddenly pop into her head, like leaving Europe, like getting her hair cut; likewise, there would be memories and fictitious scenarios—the ocean, evergreen foliage, Celestin as a handsome fiancé, or Ti-Jus, jacket draped over his shoulders like a cape, sweater sleeves rolled up . . . And the young man, as his mother imagined him, would stride among the throngs of the SUMABA, sure that people would step to one side as he passed—as they did, in fact, at the same time as eyes turned in synchrony to follow him, glued to his profile from afar, to his back, or else riveted—as if by force—to the fragile, downy relief of the ulnar artery running the length of his forearm.

The female customers, two by two, would elbow one another.

"Did you see that?"

Or each to herself:

"*O, alas! Would that he would linger . . . !*"

115

They all wished they could be crossing his path in perpetuity—being noticed by him, gazed upon, grazed by him, bumped into on purpose . . . Not knowing his real name, they would tag him with admiring sobriquets, repeated endlessly like some secret entreaty, which the more timid among them would accompany with an autarchic huddling, while the bolder made nimble advances—though most performed a mixture of both: head lowered, but giving a fiery look from underneath; hands joined together demurely, one on the other, at the center of the chest, but accompanied by an arching of the back, a spreading of the legs, a swaying of the hips that would belie the modesty of the hands' position.

During these daydreams, Bessie would sit up straight in her chair, recovering the full height and classy bearing of her better days. Whether cashing a check or making change, whether handing the umpteenth customer plastic bags or a ballpoint pen, she would beam. And each time she stopped her conveyer belt and picked up another item to scan, she would do so in such a way as to barely touch it, as if, rather than prehension, she were applying some magnetic force instead, or as if between her fingers and the objects they grasped, a layer of simple gentleness, diaphanous and subtle, was acting as an insulator.

3. 03

Documents, pills, or some utensil, she'd probably left it in the change tray, or maybe in the glove compartment, she would go out and check, and while she was at it, stop at the gas station. But it had suddenly started raining so hard that Madame Fenerolo had retreated into the supermarket for cover instead of making a dash for her car. She'd had the reflex reaction of removing her pelisse and stretching it over her head like a wide-brimmed hat, in the hope of saving her coiffure and make-up, even if it meant her new skirt would get wet. Even that didn't suffice. Not only her skirt, but the wool-and-silk blend crew-neck top she was wearing was stained with wet streaks in a matter of seconds, and even her face was streaming soon, as though she had immersed it in water. The manager kept her composure. To everyone—customers and staff alike—who saw her coming back through the door of the SUMABA in this state, not only did she bear no resemblance whatever to the disheveled woman one might have expected under these circumstances, but she was all smiles, her complexion refreshed by the cold, and her figure embellished, as though blossoming after contact with her primal element.

A long-term effect of this episode, when, later on, having dried off and redone her hair and make-up, she momentarily abandoned her battery of monitors to come mingle in the life-size, analog world of the customer, was that Madame Fenerolo seemed to shine with a special brightness, not restricted to mere appearance but singularly present in all of her being, in her fullness, along with her legs, hips, waist, buttocks, crotch—all the parts of the body that go unseen beneath a skirt, of course, but that are truly there nevertheless, just as surely as her feet were truly in her pumps; so much so, in fact, that long after she'd returned to her office and once more become a disembodied voice broadcasting over the store's loudspeakers, people were still seeking her out, raising their eyes as if to search some foliage, and at times believing they had spotted her, setting out in pursuit of a shadow, a fleeting glimmer, a mirage . . . The voice announced that a new department was soon to open. It called for extra shopping carts to be brought in from outside or asked that so-and-so go help out the cashiers. It promoted the daily specials—all frozen food on sale for one hour only, the homemade Creole-style blood sausages . . . Customer eyes fluttered, striving to visualize the words, and on that basis, reconstitute the speaker: the phonetic lengthening of *hour* in *for one hour* somehow conjured up the tapering of her legs; the syncopation of *eole* in *Creole-style* invoking the articulation of belly and thighs; or was it the cheerfulness, the bracing effect of *new department* that revived the way her two feet, all on their own, and as if making light of it all, had supported her body's upright linearity, defying gravity with each step: nimble, light, though resolute in their momentum and firmly planted on the ground at the moment of contact.

The same voice, finally, amplified and multiplied by the same loudspeakers, requested that the last customers make their way to the checkout lines. After the crowd, the void; after commotion, stillness. Soon, out in the parking lot, as daylight slowly vanished on the suburban horizon, with the company pickup trucks on one side and the manager's car on the other, wild animals alone remained in the diffused halo of streetlamps, pretending not to notice one another, observing the tenuous truce that daily precedes the night, with its lightening strikes, its processions, its abductions, death rattles, and bloodletting. Bessie waited near the Opel. The manager, now only twenty or thirty meters away, turned around in a single movement and pointed her car keys to the three-deep row of shopping carts chained to the iron grating.

"Good and tight!" she shouted, emphasizing each syllable, like the execution of a figure-skating jump with its take-off and landing.

Then, having joined cashier and car while removing her pelisse in the process, she once again whirled around to open the back door; and preparing to lay the article of clothing across the back seat, she bent over, flexing her knees without fully crouching or allowing them even the slightest deviation from their perfect pairing.

Her flexing in this fashion or twirling in place looked easy. For the manager, they were assuredly as natural as sitting on one's backside or standing on one's feet, as instinctive as—in this case—pulling at one's skirt or smoothing out its wrinkles with the palm of one's hand. Graceful gestures, in any case, easily the equal of those provoked by that morning's sudden downpour, or those that the loudspeaker voice had offered to the imagination beneath the iron girders of the SUMABA—all of which seemed necessarily to belong to a loveable person, loveable in all ways and in the strongest sense of the word *loveable*, someone who need only touch with the tip of her finger, or brush ever so lightly, or indeed merely approach the material world for its substance to spring into life.

By Thiais, however, the illusion had lifted.

It was the middle of rush hour, heading out of Paris and into the suburbs. It had started raining again. Car door to car door, bumper to bumper, vehicles of all makes, models, and sizes were creeping forward, when they weren't completely gridlocked. Occasionally, an exhaust pipe would roar or explode with impatience. Elsewhere, due either to a half-asleep motorist suddenly roused from his torpor, or to a phobic reaction to the shimmering of some puddle on the blacktop, a car would suddenly pull out of line. This would set off a chain reaction of disorderly conduct, accompanied by a concert of car horns. But the disturbance would be short-lived, as if in the surrounding gloom the drivers were even more keenly aware than in daylight of the indecency of their noises. Reduced once again to rumbling engines, alternatively idling or gearing up, gleaming with rain, haloed in fumes and the steam released continuously by their hot metal into the cold air, the long cortege of vehicles seemed resigned to an endless migration under the russet, rain-soaked, suburban sky.

In the comfort of their passenger compartments, however, people were furious. The radio confirmed it—"You're furious out there on the southbound!" In the Opel, in particular, Madame Fenerolo, in a fit of rage, went so far as to hit the off button of her car radio . . . and this made all the difference.

Switching off a car radio was a harmless gesture. A show of temper in such circumstances was perfectly understandable. Thus, the THIS in *this made all the difference* pertains not to the gesture itself, nor even to the acerbic abruptness of its execution, but to the fact that the manager had so fully and unreservedly embodied the meanness and viciousness of her gesture. The act itself had been brief. It lasted only as long as a click or a clack—"You're furious out there on the *click* . . ." Nonetheless, just as when hatred or deceit have appeared, even once, on the most beloved of faces, and that same face then becomes forever hostile and deceptive in our eyes, convincing us that it had always been thus, the THIS which the manager's act had manifested defined in advance the actions, positions, and words to follow, and indeed her entire person, and by retroactively modifying the images that she had previously generated at the SUMABA, THIS devalued those marvels into vulgar fantasies—not without their own attractions, certainly, but not even remotely loveable. Henceforward, both inside and outside the Opel, the climate degenerated—with each passing moment, the silence grew more oppressive, and then, all of a sudden, hail . . . THIS was in the air, epidemic, and THIS threatened to contaminate all persons and all matter, to infest every land, to gangrene burns and deepen wounds until all human bodies were stricken with its inhumanity. Wherever one went, whatever one did, soon dreaming would amount to nothing. However long and high the frontage, no matter how deforested the surrounding woodland, one's lookouts would be reduced to futile expectation, to pointless searching. Such that no mirage, no view anywhere in Île-de-France could console the watchers and dreamers, nor could reason still have a hope of checking the bestial momentum of the crazy avenging hordes.

3. 04

Over the days that followed, between Highway A6 and the Seine basin, the word was spreading that it would be a late spring, if spring were ever to return at all. Already, summer had been chilly, and autumn dry; and now as March was approaching, the first winter snows had yet to fall. The worst was feared for the water table. Though a lot of rain had fallen recently, it had been late in coming, and mostly in the form of sudden downpours, not penetrating enough—unbeneficial for farmland and, put starkly, symptomatic of a climate gone haywire. When the locals of Île-de-France would secretly scrutinize their peers, or gaze worriedly at their own reflections, or at the heavens, they seemed fearful of uncovering a mysterious anomaly, or of recognizing the harbingers of something irreparably life-threatening. In their cars, at home, when the weather forecast came on, they would listen to their radios, stare into their TV screens as they might once have drunk in the wisdom of a soothsayer and shared in her visions. Outdoors, pedestrians would tremble at the approach of a stranger, at the sight of a group of people moving toward them. They would avoid dark alleys, give parked campers a wide berth, likewise construction-site huts, tarpaulin-covered trailer beds abandoned by their tractors; and if they were to venture through some empty lot, they would hurry on, nervously surveying their environs, jittery and jumpy, as though a banner had flapped in the wind behind them, or the galloping hoofbeats of death personified had rung out.

Yet, as far as death, the heavens, or the water table were concerned, The Smoker and The Whistler couldn't have cared less, any more than they cared about the landscape they were passing through on the way from Corbeil to Ris-Orangis. They barely even glanced at the river that flowed on their right, at the base of the hillside, or, on their left, at the Évry plateau, where the column-like silhouette of a distant water tower rose against the light, with aerial beacons keeping constant vigil. They lent their ears neither to the cawing of crows nor to human voices, any more than to the continuous din of traffic or rustling of the wind, or to the intermittent roar of airplanes overhead. A vicious watchdog could start barking, rain could come pouring down, or a gust of winter air bring them the odor of gasoline or the smells of woodland undergrowth, and the two hikers would still continue obliviously along their path, as if deprived of their senses; the invariable brightness of their eyes betraying no one particular inner state any more than another—inebriation no more than passion, or lack of sleep, or any particular feeling besides emptiness. They walked along absentmindedly, each letting out his breath from time to time: spasmodic, like a tic. The Whistler would shoot a hoot-like whistle into the air; The Smoker would rock his head back, sometimes expelling smoke from his mouth, sometimes just steam. Occasionally they would talk. One would say, "Over at The Gardeners', the *Furreez* are nappy but happy," or "The Reef's knackered at a ramble"; the other would go "yeah," and after a brief silence, exclaim: "*Pholus*, the ever-bowl!" or "Vayshun" for *Aggravation* or just "vaysh" or "shun" . . . They rarely completed their sentences, barely articulate. Most of the time, they said nothing.

When on the outskirts of Ris they had to cross twice three lanes of national highway, they would use the footbridge. They would climb the ramp at a leisurely pace, striding forward purposefully nonetheless, and spontaneously heave themselves upward in a final effort to reach the top, a metallic platform under which an uninterrupted flow of traffic passed in a deafening roar. The suburbs extended in all directions: constructed, landscaped, variously developed depending on the sector, and diminishing in scale until they melted into the horizon. What they saw was a town, a city, two cities, three cities agglomerated, but also an isolated housing block among the fields and construction cranes; or a succession of chain-link fences, billboards, automobiles, all separated by leafless trees, and written into the same vast network of power lines and blacktopped roadways; or a freight-train yard, a housing subdivision, a soccer field, and even an office building with its sleek, mirrored walls; or a flat-topped big-box store selling light fixtures or gardening supplies. On the uplands of Évry, the aerial beacons persisted, tiny red flashes barely piercing the daylight, while the Seine continued to slip slowly toward the northwest, at first rectilinear and dull in the shadow cast by the hillside, then etching out a wide curve that glistened, segmented, in the distance by the Juvisy highway bridge, then further on by the Lyon bridge . . . But the two boys paid little attention to the landscape, any more than they had at any other time, clearly indifferent to the world of the senses, or perhaps identifying so strongly with what made up their everyday environment that they felt no need to visualize it in order to experience its presence, nor indeed to perceive it through any of their senses—just as we need not actually see the sun of this dry season weave light and shadow at our feet, nor do we need to see the rainy season's showers pelt the brownish-red puddles along the boulevard and varnish the termite mounds, nor hear its frenzied clamor strafing our roofs, because we always keep alive within us—though perhaps at the very back of our minds—the past presence of those partition screens, reddish laterite soils, and corrugated tin.

Meanwhile, somewhere else, on his way—like his two friends—to meet up with the fourth, the hulk with the comb arrived in the vicinity of their agreed-upon meeting place. He was also walking along absentmindedly, nonchalantly, though in long strides. But as he descended into the bowels of the pedestrian passage that ran under Avenue de Paris, the sloping terrain began to make itself felt, and he changed speed. Was it out of fear of sliding on the wet cement—and this would have made perfect sense—that he made up for the tenuous footing on the ramp by moving more quickly?

Was it just the childish desire to yield his entire bodyweight to the pull of the downhill slope . . . ? He ran. Such an enormous, tumbling mass made the underground passage suddenly seem lacking in width, in height; in particular lacking any escape route, or at least a recess where any hapless passersby might have found shelter. The lateral walls and ceiling shook under the repeated impact of the hulk's work boots against the ground; daylight itself fled before the recklessness of his assault; and the captive echo resounded eerily, bringing the far-off into the midst of the nearby, nesting far-flung horizons into the core of these cramped surroundings, magnifying in the cavernous space the gleeful puffing and panting that kept beat with the hulk's pace.

Back into daylight and open air, he was once again on the Mermoz side, and back in Beuilhet Alley, shortly thereafter, he met up with Ti-Jus, then The Smoker and The Whistler. And so, the four boys—together once again—idled away the time until nightfall.

They recalled the past, but with no special enthusiasm, as if what really mattered were only that they not talk about the present or future. Several times, a group incursion into the Deux-Rivières living room or kitchen brought them into contact with Celestin. Ti-Jus called his father *papa*; his friends would say *Monsieur Deux-Rivières*—a simple "Bonjour Monsieur Deux-Rivières," or "We're getting in your way, Monsieur Deux-Rivières, sorry 'bout that . . ." They turned on the TV, snickered between two mouthfuls, two gulps, turned it off. Back in Ti-Jus's bedroom, having come across some audio cassettes among the other junk piled up on the bed, they played some music.

A "Listen to that!," a "*Kyroballs!*," or a "Yeah!" stretched over three syllables, did what they could, at varying intervals, to keep the energy level high after a promising start, but enthusiasm soon waned. There was too little anger in their yelling, too little joy in their laughter, both suspiciously emanating less from their mood than a desire to pass the time. For instance, having reached for his pack of cigarettes and finding it empty, The Smoker flared up, pacing around the room, endlessly repeating the same curse words: *nepheho*, or just *pheleore* or *plasmaphele*. But his bombastic facial expressions, his pretentious intonation betrayed the artificiality of all this vehemence. And in the end, the four strapping boys didn't give away how they really felt until the afternoon had collapsed into evening, when they all started glancing at the clock-radio, each executing something akin to little warm-up exercises, like massaging an ankle or stretching out one of his fingers, showing the care and contemplation of an athlete limbering up for an Olympic event.

When the hour had come, Ti-Jus was the first to rise. He went and got some money from the family kitty, and as if it were for something trivial, informed his father.

"I'm taking some money from the kitty."

Then while preparing himself to go out, to his friends, without changing tone:

"We're out of here?"

3. 05

To this signal, the friends responded with the same "We're out of here," this time in the affirmative, adding a couple of variants, from "Bye-bye *phaï-laï*," to "Let's go, *pholo*," including "Lead the way, *phélé*, we're behind you!" They each called out a "Monsieur Deux-Rivières," by way of good-bye to Celestin, who kept silent, deaf to this brief courtesy, and deaf too to the commotion of the four boys hurtling down the stairs.

They set out for the Évry Bowling Alley, walking four abreast and laughing more readily as a foursome than each would have alone—and talking louder than a twosome would—so energized that they seemed with each step to ravage the ground with their soles, to jostle every space they entered. At regular intervals, a streetlamp set their hair aglow, or some saliva shot into the air and crash-landed on the asphalt. Past episodes were recalled: one of their prior trips to Évry, back when the Bowling Alley was a real bowling alley, a fight one day in Corbeil with The Gardeners—and speaking of The Gardeners, had The Whistler run into them lately? Yes, just this morning. Would they be there tonight? Yes, they would.

They were.

They greeted one another enthusiastically, like good friends who happened to share the same argot. The sound system was so loud they had to shout to be heard and gesticulate broadly in support of their voices.

Various bits of news were thus exchanged, greeted with "uh-huh" and "hip!," with "'rytos" with "'poddamia," half smug, half skeptical. Then, since there were no plans afoot to band together into a single group, they took leave of one another, and the Mermoz boy and affiliates went off to find seats elsewhere.

They had to slalom through chairs, tables, and drinkers before crossing the dance floor, where their bodies flashed blue, yellow, red. The Whistler poked fun at the hulk with the comb: the colors were flattering—especially the yellow, it made him look classy. The Smoker upped the ante: "Comb-Man's a real shet'!" . . . To say *shet'*, he had curled back his lips and kept his teeth clenched. To say *Comb-Man*, he had stretched out his neck . . . At first amused, even flattered, wagging his head in any case, the so-called Comb-Man's spirits soon darkened; suddenly furious as he took a seat around the little bistro table where Ti-Jus had just sat down, reinforcing his invective by flipping a phallic middle finger, he asked his taunting friends if they knew what they could do with their . . . or how they would like it if he . . . But it was time to get drinking, not to get angry. What was everyone having? The cover charge included one drink each. Who had the tickets? And finally, it would take two of them to carry it all back—bottles, cans, glasses. Who was coming along with The Smoker to the bar?

It was The Whistler, and alone with Ti-Jus, the hulk with the comb, still pissed off, said it all really pissed him off. That they called him *shet'* and *Comb-Man*, and just generally ragged on him, it pissed him off. He placed his hands palms down in front of him to keep them from shaking, pressing them to the table as if he wanted to crush it or drive it into the floor; and even though he was starting to calm down, he said again that it pissed him off.

Ti-Jus chose this moment to remind his friend of the body-search they'd all been subjected to just then at the entrance to the Alley. The bouncers had made things rather unpleasant. They had been overly zealous—and, as it happened, completely ineffectual: blind to what Ti-Jus was about to display, held tightly in his closed fist.

"Here, look."

With only the handle showing—yet still shiny, dense, weighty to the eye, still precious because of its invisible blade—the switchblade appeared, its substance seeming doubly hard by contrast with the pale, delicate epidermis of Ti-Jus's palm. The hulk was speechless. He emitted a kind of high-pitched moan, then the short fricative sound of inhaled air mixed with saliva between the teeth, eyeing the switchblade, then Ti-Jus, and again the switchblade with the same look of amazement. When he finally said something, his terse commentary consisted of few words exclaimed several times each, such as *shit, crotch,* and *buck mount*—this last in particular repeated persistently—and whose meaning was extensible enough that, depending upon the inflexion, they conveyed loathing or esteem as necessary, suitable both for badmouthing the bouncers and extolling Ti-Jus.

Back with their drinks, the two carriers were let in on the secret, so the four boys could now sit back and drink and be delighted. They smoked, they chatted. They drank again and delighted anew. But when, after music and soccer, the subject switched to girls, their mood changed.

Each was now staring stupidly at his glass, or at some imaginary point within. Their speech was broken up by long silences. Their "yeahs" and "buck mounts" sounded pensive; and while their heads rocked heavily front to back, their jaws were set sideways, as if in perpetual rumination. They talked about the girls of Ris-Orangis, then the Corbeil girls, the ones from Avron, Évry, Orly, and everywhere else: built this way, stacked that way; whether they would hang out together on the blacktop or in a muddy lot, a basement, a bus, or a train. They also talked about who saw who when, who would be seeing who again soon, who remembered what, who had a chance . . . and about a blue sweater.

So many girls, so much talk barely audible over the blasting of the sound system, this all had its effect on the hulk with the comb, so that he got up and went over to The Gardeners, who saw him approaching, more hulk than ever, looking determined. "A little while ago," he began, before continuing with "girl" and "blue" and "sitting here," then with surprise, "no? . . ." He thought she had been. His friend Ti-Jus thought so too—he had recognized her, was trying to find her, so where was she?

The Gardeners chortled in various shades of mockery. They said that the Mermoz boys must not be getting enough; that self-abuse makes you hallucinate, you know . . . One of them, however, taking a contrary position just for the hell of it, chiding his friends for their immorality—such liars!—told the hulk with the comb that yes, in fact, a girl, blue, yes, here, a little while ago; except that, here's the thing, a man—a real one—came by and picked her up—what a shame, huh . . . ?

The Gardeners became increasingly high spirited, reaching new peaks of wit and daring that culminated in the final blow: Was Ti-Jus so *pussy-whipped* that he needed a middle-man? And so arrow-headed that he'd lost all his sense . . . ? Because this girl, to tell the truth, was nothing but a *dia*, more *hippo* than *dam*, practically *shet'*—but the Mermoz boys liked *shet'*, didn't they? Just as they liked to *nick the stud*: the hulk with the comb liked that, he was a good *stud-nicker*, wasn't he . . . ?

A cloying murmur, a bland smile, and then, out of nowhere, a body swung around and a leg lashed out: with the combined plosion of broken bone and battered flesh, the Mermoz boy's work boot connected with the jaw of the nearest Gardener. A wine pitcher took flight, its contents spurting into space, and crashed to the floor after bouncing off the skull of the hulk with the comb. But, by then, the hulk had already grabbed a second joker by the collar, and while passing an arm between his victim's legs, in one swift move, lifted him up and flipped him over. He was now holding his prey parallel to the ground, the way he might have held a chainsaw in order to cut a trunk into logs or to slice some Chimera in two. But, depending on whether urgency or tactical advantage was steering him toward a defensive or dissuasive action, he handled his living load sometimes like an aegis, sometimes like a *bo*—a kind of truncheon—or else he used him as a battering ram when the time came to go on the offensive.

Despite this weaponry and its valiant deployment, the sheer number of his adversaries would inevitably have gotten the better of the hulk with the comb were it not for the timely assistance provided by the three other Mermoz boys. They rushed to their friend's side, and the scene immediately turned into a brawl, a free-for-all, where fists, keys, kicks, and head-butts soon produced cuts, bruises, fractures. No less swiftly, fear spread through the Bowling Alley. It originated at the tables immediately surrounding The Gardeners, among the witnesses in the front line who, as soon as the first Mermoz reinforcements had arrived on the scene, leaned back and turned away, as if forced by the strength of some overpowering wind. Fear was also blooming at the other end of room: not instantaneous fear, perhaps, but vague foreboding when the distant commotion first became noticeable, turning into alarm when the two bouncers burst in, then resolving into an acute anxiety that mounted as the brawl spread and the two house musclemen swept through the crowd, and finally out-and-out fear when the two bouncers—all eyes following their progress—arrived at the precise location of the fistfight, which by then was undergoing a second eruption, more furious, more disorderly than ever, and fraught now with the inevitability of catastrophe. Behind the bar, the bustling of the waiters, normally so perfunctory, had become a senseless, buzzing thrill, a barely contained response to the tumult that had now brought nearly all of their customers out of their seats. The club manager, retiring to the background behind the waiters, was fingering his cell phone with the nervousness of someone who's concluded that he should, that he'll certainly have to, but would rather not, and is putting off the decision . . . In the midst of all this, the sound system, unperturbed, continued to blast its bass tempo, powerfully modulating its upper register, its middle range, working itself into ear-splitting feedback effects. It saturated the acoustic space, so that the fight scene unfolded with neither curses nor cries, even though these were certainly being emitted by all participants: gaping wide, mouths here were nothing but wells of darkness; animated by quick contortions, moving lips seemed to accompany only a feverish chewing motion; or, when hands went to mouths to form a megaphone, they amplified nothing but their own presence. This silent grimacing—which lent the paroxysmal expressions of ritual masks to everyone's faces, and to persons in motion the frenetic appearance of worshipers in a trance, or allegories of the underworld—added its own strangeness to the violence of the fear in the room, and the brutality of the beatings being dealt out.

A random tibia caught in some wiring, or more purposefully a finger flipping a switch, finally brought the music to a stop. With this, the nature of the chaos in the room changed so much that it seemed as though everyone had been transported to a different location. People were screaming, people were moaning, people were calling out for calm, arms flailing, torsos pitching, the rest unable to budge, and likewise unable to tear their eyes away from the sparring boys. As for the fighters themselves, besides the customary grunts and groans that wrestlers and boxers deploy to enhance a hold or a hit—or those that emerge spontaneously out of pain—they added to the ambient polyphony the rather unexpected notes of their laughter. For, be they Gardeners or Mermoz boys, they were all laughing—and not only out of sarcasm, to add insult to the injury of a bouncer laid low, or more generally to mock a vanquished adversary, but also because they were quite simply having fun getting bashed or doing some bashing, however much damage it caused. A young man flat on his stomach on the floor, clumsily trying to crawl away from the battlefield, his body bruised and beaten; another holding his bloody head in both hands; a third trying, with his one uninjured arm, to lift a friend too groggy to even get to his knees all the way to his feet—every one of them, as dazed, one-armed, bloodied, and bruised as they were, every one of them was laughing, mouth gaping and shoulders shuddering, the vibratory expulsion of their breath resounding; while others, more loquacious, uttered with increasing speed and ever-higher pitch some series of words until these merged into a kind of extended diphthong that prolonged the crescendo well beyond any single lexical item. In this way, because

The Smoker's foot now formed an impossible angle with his ankle, this mangled limb became the laughing stock of The Whistler and the hulk with the comb: they said "wrist," or what remained in their mumbling of the word *wrist*, and the cripple likewise said "wrist"—but it was clearly his ankle that they were all pointing to, his own extravagant ankle that he was considering, half astonished, half amused—as if prudishness or some superstition had prohibited them all from naming any part of the lower body.

A short while later, nevertheless, back out in the cold and the night, the same cripple said "balls," said "dickhead," said "asshole" followed—or not—by "buck mount." He asked to be carried gently, and for his beast of burden to walk slowly.

"Easy, easy," grumbled the hulk with the comb. Did The Smoker think he was light or something . . . ? And as for slowing down or speeding up: didn't he see the pulsating electric blue aura of rotating police lights over there? Didn't he hear the shrill stuttering of sirens . . . ?

The Smoker persisted with his dirty words—multiples of "asshole," of "shit-maker," of "shaft." But a core of hilarity continued to cut short his breath and rasp his voice; so that when he rebuked The Whistler for fighting so half-heartedly, or Ti-Jus for not unsheathing his secret weapon, each of them inferred that homage was actually being paid to the intrepid actions of the first, and that, for better or for worse, it was generally approved that the latter's switchblade should be held in reserve for a later date.

3. 06

Certain regulars at the Évry Bowling Alley preferred never to mention what had gone on in front of their eyes that evening, withholding the event for memory alone, like an experience too intimate to be shared with anyone, and too physical, at any rate, for words to relate anything that might approach the truth. Images of bruised flesh, of blood, of exposed bone and lips contorted by laughter pursued them into sleep and their waking hours both, each time confronting them with the brutal fact that other people could be what they themselves were not. They experienced this as a vexation, embittered that their own natures weren't monstrous enough to allow for such unbridled behavior, even if this behavior meant abandoning all human reason, as had the Mermoz boys and The Gardeners.

Other witnesses more inclined to telling tales gladly recalled the havoc of flying objects and swinging appendages; the composite resonance of a given impact, at once thud, slap, thrust, and crack; or the heavy, slack collapse of a suddenly reified body. The more stories they told, the more their earlier fear evolved into vainglory, when it didn't lapse into nostalgia. Then, many a listener having become storyteller in turn, as the memory gradually degenerated into gossip, the initial thrill of the few who'd actually been present at the brawl turned at last into the hostility of the many toward persons they had never seen.

Such a feeling spread unimpeded all throughout Île-de-France. They found fertile ground in many minds. In Ris-Orangis, in the Vallon neighborhood, and particularly at the apartment complex of the same name, the security guard displayed this new antagonism with special fervor. "They," he would say—or "those people," or "those," never specifying the referent except to point a malicious chin toward some vague horizon. He would approach the residents, delay them outside in the freezing cold or in the overheated hallway: did they know how vicious *they* were? what a nuisance *those people* had become . . . ? And look how *they* stood, and how *they* looked, and how *they* pissed . . .

Thus, in the rear building, she about to exit, he having just entered, a young, high-breasted lady and a frail old gentleman were compelled to linger between the keypad-guarded glass door and the glass door with the intercom. The young lady was holding her car keys. She was clutching them tighter and tighter in her fist, and would soon press them, shivering, against her throat. The old gentleman was nodding his head, without making explicit whether this sign of approval was meant as sympathy with his neighbor's state of agitation or as fuel for the security guard's inflammatory speech.

"You'll see," insisted the latter, like one who had seen more than his share of trouble in this life, thank you very much.

And growing exasperated:

"And so many of them . . . !"

Mouth surly, eye cantankerous.

"And they make such a racket . . . !"

Now mere inches away from his listeners, as if to share some secret with them, he spoke in a whisper while casting a sideways glance at the mirrors on either side of them, multiplying the lobby into an ever-shrinking infinity.

The building was quiet. One could hear only the distant, intermittent clinking of dishes and silverware being emitted at each floor, or perhaps, every so often, the muffled call of someone's name, or, more muted still, the message playing on an answering machine. Outdoors, dissipating the early nightfall, the street lamps in the residents' parking lot mingled their glow with the footpath lights in the garden, thereby conserving the colors and forms of any local, terrestrial objects, while the din of the traffic on the Avenue de Paris raised a wall of sound—climbing toward the sky rather than descending the embankment—on the near side of which there was still room enough for silence and even individuated sounds in the continuum of quiet. In short, a kind of harmony prevailed, or at least an orderliness that reassured the residents as well as the security guard that the days to come would be identical to the previous ones. Yet, the young lady looked worried all of a sudden. She had brought one hand up to her throat and held the other in front of her, fingers outstretched on the same vertical plane, palm pressed against the void as if to signify "Hush! Listen . . ." The frail old gentleman not only interrupted his nodding, but ceased all movement, and just as his neighbor was doing, stood there frozen in place, face raised to the chrome brackets of the drop ceiling. But the security guard, too worked up to notice—or even want to notice—these signs, carried on with his diatribe. He made reference to hygiene, to tradition, spoke of the very soil of Île-de-France, how certain people were purposely sowing their seeds in order to put down roots; and as if this word summed up all his previous statements, he added *pissers*, repeated it—"pissers . . . !" After which, needing to catch his breath, or perhaps petrified by some phantasmagorical apparition, he in turn fell silent and stood stock-still, eyes glazed, wide open, deactivated—same as those of the two residents, and the same too as any eyes when imagination rather than sight has begun to determine meaning, or when the ears, on high alert, require that nothing visual be allowed to distract them.

Confirmed by the infinite reflecting mirrors set face to face in the foyer, this frozen scene seemed now to be separate from the rest of the residence, having abandoned it to its own devices, leaving it unguarded, open to the wind and wild animals, to all and sundry. New notions prowled the area, images, quasi-real persons, liable to venture where normally a "Who goes there?" would have prevented them from getting in. On the private grounds of the Vallon Apartments, detritus could now roll by with impunity, pushed along by the same gust of wind that would festoon the young pine trees with triumphant new wreckage: newspapers, bits of rag, plastic bags, and even long filaments of jute or of fiberglass, each clump looking like a raw chunk of scalp. Or perhaps the intruding *all and sundry* would only include a few boys—but big ones, strong-limbed, hulking and violent enough to cause as much damage as a horde. They would wreck the lawn and the residential walkways with their stampeding. They would overturn the cars parked in the visitors' lot, gleefully setting them ablaze. Or stationed at a certain distance from one another, in a random distribution, they would piss together, attempting at the same time to catch each other's eye and conversing merrily in their argot; and more concerned with their words than their deeds, a living insult to the local mindset, they would seem to be off in their own world, unconcerned by material existence and their own organisms, unmindful even of their own micturition, despite the cataract-like noise their urine would make when it struck the ground, as if to spite the cold, creating a long plume of vapor between the sprinkled ground and their bare penises.

A car arrived, saving the apartment complex from wrack and ruin, dispelling in the process any idea of those gleeful pissers. It was an Opel. A fur-lined raincoat was carefully laid out across the back seat, while the front passenger seat was occupied by a box of freshly processed foods. Madame Fenerolo was at the wheel.

"Yes, thank you, I'd like that very much," she said to the security guard, who had leapt up to offer his assistance.

Then, to the lady with the keys, "Good evening"; and, locking up her private garage space while another driver was opening his own, two or three comments on the traffic, before renewed wishes finally for a pleasant evening.

The security guard escorted Madame Fenerolo into the rear building, bearing her box with the kind of pride felt by a starlet's porter or the retinue of a Generalissimo from the days of yore. Their environs hailed them as conquerors: door after door opened before them, the lateral mirrors cloning their twosome into an army. Hardly had the button been pushed than the elevator had arrived, and, of its own volition, opened the way into the gleaming recessed lights and polished scent of its cabin.

The box was getting heavy, however. Having failed initially to lift it high and hold it close enough, the porter was about to give up.

"Leave it, that's fine," said the manager. "I'll manage, put it down right there."

The security guard ignored this order. In one breath, while designating the buttons for the various floors with an urgent glance, he merely requested: "Can you . . . ?"

The manager hesitated, a mere formality—"You sure . . . ?" But by the time she said *all right*—"Well, all right. That's really nice of you"—she'd already pressed 5 with the end of her gloved index finger.

3. 07

Eight days had elapsed since a certain incident, and during train rides and pedestrian outings, from suburb to suburb, each of the boys had chanced to observe a clear change in Ti-Jus. Only the hulk with the comb denied the obvious. The Smoker pointed out that their friend no longer listened to music, The Whistler that he seemed oblivious to their jokes, their insults, their questions, that his voice seemed extinguished for good, while the hulk retorted that *A*, that wasn't true, and *B*, music or no music, Ti-Jus still wore his headphones around his neck, keeping his Walkman in his pocket, just like he always had, and *C*, he had never exactly been the talkative type, had he, and anyway, what, nobody's allowed to change around here anymore?

But The Whistler and The Smoker still hounded the dissenter. Half attempting to convince him, half riling him for the fun of it, they pressured him to open his eyes, saying he was blind not to see what was going on, and as they gave him the finger or waved one of his crutches at him, they would call him *mule* or *lemu* or *throatlatch* or just *tlatch*, the way other friends in conversation might call one another prick or jerk. But even in the face of all the evidence, however persuasive, the hulk had too strong a feeling for the permanence of his friend's identity to acknowledge these occasional alterations, and thus he persisted in his denial: Ti-Jus was Ti-Jus; Deux-Rivières with *D* as in Dodo, ding-dong or Demeter; Teej, if they liked, but nobody other than himself, and same as the old Ti-Jus ever was.

But however impervious he may have been to their arguments, however indifferent to objective fact, the hulk with the comb, by virtue of his own behavior, demonstrated the very same new situation that his words strove to deny. Some mimetic instinct drove him more than ever to take it all out on empty cans, which he crushed between his powerful fingers, or else on the pavement, which his work boots struck as though trying to split open the asphalt, or else, most furiously, on the very space before him, reaching to the four corners of the horizon, which he battered with all his might, chest thrust forward, scorning distance as he chewed up the kilometers, one by one.

Because this was also how his model behaved.

For a week now, in fact, Ti-Jus had been the perfect picture of a disjointed body: fists and feet, torso and jaw each working separately to molest the world. If he ever did happen to come together to form one compact individual, it was an exceptional occurrence and resulted from the shock of some outside stimulation, the smell of wool or of skin, a certain tone of voice, a silhouette, or even a mere flash of blue he thought for an instant looked familiar. This would happen regularly on the Paris-Corbeil train, during the station stop at Maisons-Alfort, or when the train would cross the Lyon Bridge. Then, away from the train, away from the station or the bridge, there were banks of the Seine at Ris-Orangis. Ti-Jus went down to the water more often than he once had. There, he discovered an interesting nook from which poles, buildings, and indeed all signs of human existence were concealed by the blackish vegetation on either shore, where the river one could see flowing through the virgin landscape looked like some other river, Île-de-France some other isle, in some other country—an older one, perhaps, that they had seen once before, seen for the first time. But although resuscitated by this framing effect, and seconded by the constancy of the celestial geometry and of the flat scent of river water, pristine moments such as this—already fragile in the olden days—were even more so today, as fleeting as those dearly departed dead whose friendly shadows visit us from time to time, but which the least false move or slightest exclamation will send fleeing, such that we can't enjoy their renewed company without also feeling the sickening presence of nothingness.

Anyway, the girl in the blue sweater was insisting that her girlfriend come along.

"Come on, already!" she nagged at her, quadrupling the duration of *on* and dropping an octave for *already*.

She was tapping her foot, shouting orders, threats, and insults such as "bitch" or "back mount." The next moment, having assumed her sweetest, most wretched manner, she begged:

"You gotta come with!"

The other resisted: "I don't feel like it." Or more caustic: "Scratch my brillo," or "scuff the muff."

She did finally give in, though not without the girl in the blue sweater having to drag her by the arm to get her moving.

It involved taking the train. As often as possible. Hanging out in the last car of the Paris-Corbeil. Strolling through the Gare de Lyon. Scouring Juvisy for a certain bar whose name both the Maison-Alfort girls had forgotten.

In any event, they did remember the Évry Bowling Alley, and knew by simple deduction that the place bearing this name was located in Évry.

They showed up there one evening.

To any boorish remarks, compliments, or other come-ons, they retorted so sharply that all the local big mouths and tough guys beat hasty retreats. This spunkiness, quite apart from the bloom of their youth and natural charm, won over one of the barmen. Each got a double drink, free of charge, a Coke for the first, and strawberry milk shake for the second. "So, little ladies," he said—what brought them to the Bowling Alley? Were they looking for anyone in particular . . . ? Then he, after cross-examination and descriptions, replied oh yes, he'd seen them all right, seen quite a bit of them in fact, that the previous evening the four guys had made something of a scene, had been seen by quite a few people, and that these were boys they'd probably be better off forgetting, but oh well, love and all that . . . He could understand. Especially since the hulky one was a real hulk, and the hunky one a real hunk . . . Anyway, there you have it. *Mermoz, Ris-Orangis*. With that, they should be able to track them down with no problem.

The next day, the trip from the Ris train station to the Mermoz Projects felt interminable to the two *Maisonnaise* girls. One was cold, out of breath, hated walking. The other stopped every so often and turned around to shout, "Are you coming or not?" Or simply raised her head, and as if addressing the birds of the air instead of the straggler, shouting, "What do you think of him?" Her friend didn't bother replying. Neither one said anything for a while, the only sound coming from the repeated squeaking of their shoes or the rolling of pebbles catapulted unexpectedly by the force of a footfall. Vehicles at rest along the sidewalks, streetlamps extinguished, apartment buildings and other houses set in silent disarray, away from the narrow street—everything on either side of the two walkers seemed to be slumbering in broad daylight, unaffected by the nearby roar of the highway, belonging to a space entirely separate from the surround sound of suburban Paris traffic.

This isolation came to an end. The narrow street opened into a large intersection, and a general transformation increased the ambient noise and broadened the sky until suddenly the here became fused with its surroundings near and far. The girls had to skirt the traffic flow, seek out a stepping stone, make a dash for a pedestrian island, pause, then make another dash. They had to get their bearings on yet another map—"Where are we?" . . . Climb a slight incline—that was it, "Right there, no?" . . . Finally, once past the icy shadow of the northern façade, and a blustery final esplanade, they were at last within the Mermoz Projects.

When the girl in the blue sweater caught sight of him, Ti-Jus was standing in front of "Le Beuilhet," the local bar-tobacconist's, at the opposite end of Beuilhet Alley. One foot tucked under a buttock, sole and jeans pressed against a parked car, he was idly fiddling with the wire leading from his earphones to his Walkman and, without actually whistling, was pursing his lips into a whistling position. He was far away; several passersby, as well as two or three stationary clusters of people, should all—according to the laws of perspective—have taken up more space in the *Maisonnaise*'s visual field. In her mind, however, he appeared to tower over everyone else in view, seemed so close that she reflexively withdrew her arm so as not to touch him prematurely. Then, having turned once again to her girlfriend—but her pelvis restive, legs itching to spring forward, and voice barely able to contain her euphoria:

"Come have a look!"

From that day forward, his hair and his skin would come into contact with her clothes, her undergarments, her bare flesh. He pointed out some windows to her: all afternoon that apartment would be free; she should use the stairs; he, on the other hand, would take a less direct route . . . She went up. From the inside, he opened the door on the landing, and now the girl in the blue sweater was moving about comfortably in a three-room-plus-kitchen apartment off Stairwell G, Mermoz Projects, less curious about the apartment itself than about what went on there. She wanted to know exactly where Ti-Jus lived, whether he often squatted in other apartments in the projects and how he managed to get inside this one. Barely pivoting his shoulders, he pointed to the window behind him. The girl, then: wasn't that dangerous . . . ? An absentminded wag of the head said no. And her again: but seriously . . . ! he might have slipped, been seen from the outside, been the target of some sniper—and her concern suddenly switched to another object: "I talk too much, don't I . . . ?"

This interrogative statement stood without a response. Silent, the questioned party continued gazing at the questioner. He inspected a lid, a brow, the nose, the lips, the eyes, determined, one might have said, to itemize the face in such a way as to grasp the whole in each of her tiniest features. And when he finally did speak a few words, rather than picking up the conversation where it had left off, he seemed almost to be pursuing a private train of thought aloud. His words were of the *beautiful, pretty, nice* variety, perfectly straightforward, and arranged rather prosaically at that. In any other situation, they would have sounded false. But because the mouth pronouncing them belonged to Ti-Jus, and because a long silence had preceded them—just as it sometimes takes nothing more than a foreign accent to make a commonplace sound like a pearl of wisdom, nothing more than a brief hesitation for the desperate groping of memory to sound clearly amid the ruins of some forgotten idiom—despite their triteness, the words had charm, and delighted the girl in the blue sweater.

She wanted, therefore, to take things further.

Whether it was her or him that took the initiative or made the request, he lifted her off the ground and they moved from room to room, not at the pace of ordinary domestic business but literally racing, heedless of what might get knocked over in their path, fearing nothing that could have stopped them, as if henceforth all the space they wanted was theirs for the taking. Feather-light in the arms of the Mermoz boy, the girl was being held, supported, only by the back of her neck, an upper thigh, an armpit, with her limbs left free to resist the pull of gravity, her head floating, weightless. All this upheaval meant that, in exchange, the upper torso of the Mermoz boy had to remain perfectly still, and that his gaze had to be riveted to that of the girl in his arms. Without this sustained supervision, this fixed attention, their frail, unstable unit would certainly have been shattered, dislocated, and the unbounded space in which they were moving would have been reabsorbed by the three-room-plus-kitchen habitat, Ti-Jus liable once again to bump into the walls.

They lingered, then at nightfall of that winter's day, they had to start thinking about vacating the premises—yet they lingered still, while outdoors, mingling with the gloom, *THIS* was lurking in Beuilhet Alley. On their way to the train station or returning from the nearest bus stop, about to go into the café-tobacconist's or about to arrive at their stairwell bearing bags of groceries for dinner, the locals were all feeling its presence. Even though they were talking about other things or refraining from speech entirely, they were all thinking about it. Some even tried to articulate it. An outstretched arm, palm open heavenward, as if they'd been called upon as witnesses to some brazen offense, they pointed west to where the light was fading; or, index fingers pointing to the overflowing contents of two or three trash bags they were carrying in one hand, they seemed to be indicting some piece of cardboard packaging, some throw-away container, or blaming a six-pack of cans all stamped with the same expiration date. They wagged their heads slowly from left to right, left to right: "What a waste . . . !"

Half-dressed again, Ti-Jus and the girl in the blue sweater were looking out the window. The voices of Beuilhet Alley rose and echoed, allowing the pair to make out bits of distinct conversation against the background brouhaha of the suburb, with words like *throw-away*, or *stop*, or *expiration date* resonating like a sorrowful omen. Stricken in their idyllic setting, dismayed at the spread of *THIS*, the two squatters behind the windowpane faced the outside world with the same stern brow, the same posture of disillusionment: twins, for one exceptional instant; their similitude more powerful than their gender difference or disparity in size.

3. 08

We hear it, we alone, a muffled stirring in the body's prison, an utterance anxious for release from our flesh, but that we retain, captive, for although we'd like to believe it belongs to us, or is part of ourselves, we suspect it to have been implanted deep within us by some malign force—a force that has always reigned there, supreme, or else, via some ruse, which has insinuated itself gradually, and now rules incognito. Should this utterance happen to escape, suddenly inhabiting the open air, resounding in our own voice, we would fail to recognize it, would grow afraid, feel ashamed, as though we had forgotten how to use language; or else, if we were able to puzzle out the meaning of those sounds, we would find that we had been reproducing the very same words that reveal us to be rough beasts, compounding our shame—and the fear that would soon moisten our skin and make our hair sticky would indeed bring out our most animal odors.

This is why we keep quiet, why we endure the visceral dilations and constrictions, the spasms, the feelings of stifling, and, in general, all the varied frustrations occasioned by suppressed speech; why we identify not with the animals that speak, but rather with our own muteness, as well as with certain sensations and sounds: the blowing of the wind around our male bodies, the sharp, hurried hammering of our steps beneath us, the eruption of our urine, its drumming against the metallic flooring or doormats.

This identification provides some comfort, but earns us only a short respite. Deep within us, the throbbing sensation reappears—one that both urges us on and impairs our capacity to judge whether, faced with *THIS*, our silence is an act of dignity or of craven submission. We question our insides, alarmed to experience them as strangely animal; we wonder at the shadow we cast, at its excessiveness. We strain to reassure ourselves with the sight of our prehensile fingers, with the memory that we'd once been loquacious. Then, prone by turns to greater or lesser anxiety, in the end we remain uncertain as to what silence or speech even mean.

Likewise, as *THIS* spread, the inhabitants of the Mermoz Projects, divided at first between the talkative and the taciturn, leaned increasingly toward a unanimous ignorance as to how they should react, what they wanted to be. Only a few dogged optimists were spared these pangs of doubt, relying on the lengthening of the days to put the future off indefinitely; the others were in despair. Evenings weighed especially heavy. People hurried up the stairwells, skin buzzing with terror at being submerged in darkness; or if by some chance the timer that ran the stairwell lights happened to be working, they worried it would stop again without warning, and at each landing, as a mindless precautionary measure, they would press the button yet again. Once home, they would likewise rush to switch on the lights. So as to ward off the incursion of any noxious darkness from the outside, blinds were lowered and shutters shut, where there were shutters, or at very least, curtains were drawn. But this proved inadequate. The sight of a mere patch of shadow on the wall turned grown men's legs to jelly. Children would wail, flailing at the invisible arm that was pushing them aside, while in a ludicrous gesture of self-protection, their mothers would hold their heads in both hands, convinced that Night Itself was about to grab hold of their hair and never let them go.

At the Deux-Rivières apartment, Bessie was talking about cyclones. Just before one descended, she said, you would feel the same universal depression—the same menacing immobility of the air, the same suspension of life. She called on Celestin as a witness, but got nothing except a tired look that seemed like the mute reiteration of the words she had just uttered: "suspension of life," "suspension of life."

Every once in a while, a blown transformer or a downed cable would knock out the power for the entire sector. A blackout like that was rare, and when it did happen, power-company technicians would rush to the scene and get things up and running again in short order. But this one lasted. Prevented from sewing, though she had only just resumed work on the Fenerolo trousers, Bessie took this event as a dire omen, something like the result of a curse. She thought of the manager, at Vallon, and of *THIS*, of the SUMABA and of Ti-Jus as a child, and of Ti-Jus grown up. There was a lump in her throat. Her stomach hurt.

A candle was lit, then another, and still another. By the hundreds, soon, isolated flames could be seen in the windows of the Mermoz Projects, giving off an eerie glow. Each one flickered, fragile, too feeble to join with its nearest neighbor's halo. Kitty-corner to the southern façade of the projects, on the sunset side, the dark silhouette of the local shopping center rose like a black burial mound, or a citadel in ruins, and the remainder of the ground between Beuilhet Alley and Avenue de Paris looked like a dangerous no-man's-land, over which the faceless gazes of the blackout zone stared out at the illuminated world. They looked like a community of ghosts being held against their will, with their sick, their dying, their dead—frightened by the belligerent splendor of the electricity laying siege to their homes, trapping them within their own walls. Any moment now, the light outside would launch its decisive assault. Or, after an interminable blockade, after terror and thirst, hunger and humiliation, the besieged would perish, little by little.

Instead of which, the power came back on. The sewing machine could run again, and if not that same night, then the next day, everything got finished, including the trousers. But despite the twinned return of electrical current and daylight, the air and life itself remained congealed. At the Deux-Rivières apartment, Celestin spent his time sitting in the kitchen, fuzzy-headed, getting up only to drag himself over to the window and press his forehead ominously to the cold pane. Even Ti-Jus was in a bad mood. As for Bessie, straining to make at least one voice heard, she chose her words with extraordinary care, as if selecting the least offensive at the expense of certain others that she would have been afraid to pronounce or hear. More than once, facing Ti-Jus, she suddenly interrupted what she was saying to him; and when, exceptionally, the son looked as though he wanted to say something in turn, his anxious mother held her breath, or even found some excuse to end the conversation before he could set anything irreversible in motion.

And yet, what was to happen happened nonetheless.

Ti-Jus in his room, Bessie in the kitchen with Celestin, an offer was shouted from one room to the next that went unanswered and, sealed off from any of the apartment's inhabitants, hovered strangely in a kind of inter-space. The thing that had been said was there, inherent to the living room—without anyone seeming to have actually spoken it—turning the ambient air as dense as the breath of prophecy. To be reunited with this utterance, mother and son would soon make their entrances simultaneously. They would converge in silence on the same place they had left behind a moment before, would take up the same face-to-face position, he upright and grave, she on the verge of collapse. Nothing new would be said. But the utterance would continue to echo, more vividly, somehow more eloquent for having two flesh-and-bone beings near it now, making the seriousness of the events to come, as well as the sorrow that would ensue, all the more tangible.

3. 09

For the occasion, as when one purifies or primps oneself before a great event, Ti-Jus shaves, showers, and will momentarily pick out his best clothes. When he returns to his room, wrapped in a towel that barely conceals him from navel to knees, his wet feet leave tracks on the mosaic parquet. Bessie chides him for this, and for the dirty clothes left behind in a ball on the bathroom floor, and for the sink left unrinsed. She sighs, lets her arms drop to her side, her head tip toward her chest, her trunk collapse in on itself, more weary than annoyed, expressing her disapproval perhaps only to stifle her graver concerns.

At the sound of the doorbell, then the greeting issued by the hulk with the comb, Bessie goes to open the door and without waiting for the question that customarily follows "Hello," she responds with, "He's in there." The hulk follows Ti-Jus's liquid tracks to the boy's room, while avoiding stepping in them. He smiles at the thought of the wool cap he's wearing, at his shaved head, at the idea of the switchblade in his pocket, and at the surprise Ti-Jus will display at all this novelty. But he's hardly across the threshold when he sees the surprise is on him. He didn't know Ti-Jus owned this bright yellow sweater, any more than these slashed jeans; and as familiar as he is with the leather jacket, for the moment laid out on the bed—as if on show for all to admire—its texture has never appeared so animal to him, nor its color so scarlet.

Meanwhile, without reacting in any overt way to his visitor's arrival, Ti-Jus continues to get ready. Is it the rigorous economy of his movements . . . ? Less naked than when he exited the shower, he's giving off a rawer power, a violence more visceral, cruder than ever, as if from head to toe, in his clothing now, he were going to become nothing more than a force of will, or a desire, or a delirium in progress—in any event, unstoppable. He empties the pockets of one jacket and, solemnly self-assured, transfers the contents to the one he will be wearing. Keys, ID, change, switchblade, each is put in its place. And when in triumph a second knife is shown to him—"Look at this!"—he pays no attention.

The friend, good-natured, not obstinate as a rule, is neither offended nor discouraged by this chilly welcome, and says how much he likes the jacket—its red leather, its shoulder guards, its cuffs. He nuances: "Lavender." Corrects: "Indigo." Adds: "Or maybe," but goes no further in his search for the *mot juste*, and in the same breath: "So where are we going?"

A silence then. The two boys in the room remain motionless, one watching, instinctively imitating the other, who, his mind busy till now planning things to come, apparently requires this moment of inertia before falling back into step with the present. Bessie and Celestin are keeping quiet too, as though participating in this scene at a distance. The father in the kitchen is standing with his face to the wall, one shoulder lower than the other, one arm reaching toward the floor—carrying what weight? The mother in the living room is staring at the package on the table in the dining area, awaiting only the moment of delivery. The discretion of its occupants serves to highlight the apartment's dreariness: a place that even neighboring sounds forsake in favor of ever more distant spaces, until they merge with the far more distant noises, just as the surrounding landscape abandons it to its solitude, always fleeing its environs for the distant space where urban sprawl meets the curved horizon.

In this context of dereliction, when he learns that Ti-Jus has some business to attend to without him, the hulk with the comb can hardly believe it: "Come aaaaahn!" . . . Next he attempts a decisive "I'm coming along," then retreats to a humbler, pleading "Well, are we buddies or aren't we?" Finally, not without some embittered frowning and a sigh of exasperation over these negotiations, he agrees to relinquish his beautiful new switchblade.

And so they're off.

Their steps resound in the stairwell, then the ample vibrations of the lobby door downstairs as it slams shut automatically. From her window, Bessie watches the two young men as they gradually shrink out of sight. They've taken the shortcut to Vallon, while she, recalling the previous evening's blackout, senses some impending misfortune, and wishes now she'd demanded they take the usual route. She's upset, shaking even—though she also feels pride at the sight of her big boy walking as he does, back straight, head high—like a handsome, grown man.

Just like Bessie, though quite differently involved, not a few Mermoz girls stationed at their windows watch the two boys as they recede into the distance. They're watching for the moment when—without seeming to do so on purpose, or even noticing that they're doing it—the boys move forward in step, bending a leg in unison and simultaneously stretching out the other, together raising a foot, extending it forward, pressing it to the ground, and so on, giving the impression of a single individual in motion. Charmed by what they see, the girls are nonetheless overcome by a dusky melancholy. They grumble at how deep space is, how short the minutes and seconds, frustrated not to be able to contemplate Ti-Jus up close and for a longer time. Why is he already so far away . . . ? They imagine his return, his gradual approach, his touch. They wonder: could a boy so *physical* be capable of feeling?—and, for that matter, should they be wishing that he could . . . ?

3. 10

Over at Vallon, the nonchalant girl and her two girlfriends raise their heads toward Avenue de Paris with a jolt. The screeching tires, car horns, and the concert of shouting voices cause them to assume there has been an accident, and for a few moments, they think that Ti-Jus might be carrying a casualty—injured, or even dead—in his arms. Clouds, darker from west to east, and broken up into multiple structures, allow sunlight to pass obliquely, imprinting the ground with the two walkers' silhouettes—though these images look as though under threat by the wind, incessantly transmuting, quivering and wavy, moving alternatively toward and away from the bodies they act to extend, in the same way that a dancer's veil might be flung into the air, shivering and wrapping around itself before being thrown once again.

One of the young girls claims that these particular shadows have special qualities. In addition to being impervious to pain, they're nimble, almost imperceptible, and therefore harmless. At which the nonchalant girl shrugs: "All shadows are like that . . . !" The other is unconvinced. She pouts in disbelief, glancing at the third girl to solicit her support. But the third girl's mind is elsewhere. "They're going to pass right by us," she predicts, excited at the prospect—and her girlfriends start teasing her: isn't she afraid of being knocked over, trampled? how would she like it if they kidnapped her . . . ? Yet now, having arrived at a place where the terrain is once again flat and solid underfoot, the soft, sloping terrain behind them—like pilgrims driven by the long distances they'd walked and the approach of dusk to take some rest—the two boys come to a halt. The hulk with the comb takes a look around, vaguely curious as to this new setting. He points eastward where night has nearly fallen, and in an aside, too softly to be heard, or in any case too softly to expect a response, he asks whether that's the direction of Évry, Corbeil, and the Coudriers Projects . . . Louder now, he shouts, "It's a hazelnut tree," which he further explains with "The word *coudrier*, it means hazelnut tree," before pursuing the subject further with "Can you pronounce -*drier* as one syllable?" He tries it, and it's as though his mouth is full of some sticky substance, impossible to deglutinate: "-*drier*" . . . But hazelnuts and deglutition are quickly forgotten: he remarks with conviction that you feel the cold more when you stand still, that there'll be frost tonight, for sure, even if the temperature hasn't hit freezing yet—and in reaction either to the temperature or to the auto-suggestion produced by his ruminations, he crosses his arms over his chest and, hugging his shoulders, rubs them in order to stop shivering.

While this is going on, and not without extreme care, Ti-Jus sets his package on the ground. With a twig broken off a low branch having been employed as a boot scraper, he's set about removing the mud clots from his sneakers. Seeing this, his friend is surprised: "What are you doing . . . ?" He laughs, as if thinking, "He's really something else!" or "No, but seriously, Teej, sometimes you just . . . ," while he himself proceeds to clean his boots as well. This cleaning operation now doubled, and taking into account the silence in which it's being conducted, and the duration of the operation, the exact site of the de-mudding becomes an autonomous zone within the neighborhood, a micro-territory sheltered from what's considered common practice elsewhere, cut off from all current events except this innocent activity, for which it serves as the temporary theater.

Emboldened by this momentary period of peace, the young girls draw nearer to the young men, gingerly, and are soon settling in right next to them. Without a word spoken, one of them sets her face in a seductive pout, the two others sucking on a wisp of hair and chewing bubble-gum, respectively, all three observing with interest how, off and on, little bits of clay are being flung into the air, how the large male bodies bend forward ever so slightly in perfect balance, each with a foot raised to about groin level, soles pointing up. Time unfolds smoothly, with only the sound of the work and the movement of the workers, until the nonchalant girl begins bobbing her head and humming a tune.

As if this was all he had been waiting for to show his disapproval of the childish threesome's presence, the hulk with the comb digs a heel into the ground and stands straight up. He flares his nostrils, sets his jaw, and scans the sky in exasperation. For a moment, he even seems on the verge of smacking the unwelcome trio, or at least yelling at them. But seeing how calm Ti-Jus has remained throughout, he manages to restrain himself, limiting his bullying to a nasty glare and his verbal abuse to a prolonged exhalation.

From then on, the girls abandon their inhibitions. The girl with the gum, in particular, after bursting bubble upon bubble, has stretched a long, rubbery cord of the stuff from her mouth, letting it swing in the breeze, like a fragile, pink climbing vine.

"I'm cutting it!" the girl next to her threatens jokingly.

The bubble-gum girl pretends she's really being threatened. She cries out in protest, to the extent her clenched teeth will allow, while turning her head away to flee the two scissoring fingers relentlessly advancing through space toward their target. Then, stopping the game all of a sudden, she takes a nimble step toward the hulk with the comb: would he like some bubble gum . . . ?

She's raised serene eyes and extended a firm arm, not intimidated in the least by the boy's type, nor his size—while he, on principle, grumbles a bit, but in the end accepts the offer. And as if this gesture had just sealed a pact that granted her whatever she might desire, the girl immediately demands that the hulk with the comb carry her on his shoulders, and that he blow a bubble-gum bubble, that he lend her his wool cap, and that he go ask Ti-Jus for a lock of his hair for her . . . The hulk hesitates. Undecided, in a crouched position with his arms dangling, like someone ready to make a standing jump, or simply looking awkward, he frowns, and then issues a few conciliatory words such as *neez', ixion, dubblepone.*

OK, says the bubble-gum girl.

Her girlfriends can't believe their eyes—she took a big risk, and won big!

"Is she getting beasty on the homeboy or what?"

"Who said she can't horse, girl?"

"Check out the Fuzz!"

3. 11

Ti-Jus—between surly security guard and hulk with comb—walks at such an even pace, holding his upper body so erect, that his legs appear both stationary and elevated, barely touching the ground, like a horseman riding impeccably in his saddle, or a skater, having attained top speed, freewheeling along the asphalt. The three girls are in agreement that he's come to deliver something. Two of them even claim to know where and what, ready to proclaim the identity of the addressee and the nature of the goods delivered, but too excited to stifle a laughing fit before the *suit* of pantsuit, and the *nero* of *Fenerolo*. Then, after this token demonstration of their divining powers, retaining only a hint of the Pythian frenzy in their movements and elocution, they revert to the recent past to compare today's heroes with those of the previous day—the descent from the mound, the crossing of Avenue de Paris, and the package being carried all being contrasted with counterparts seen on an episode of some TV adventure series.

Meanwhile, boys and guard have just entered the rear building, the security door closing with a click. Bubble-gum girl puts on a weepy face, a tragedy mask with a half-smile; she intertwines her fingers while moaning emphatically, supported in this display by one of the other girlfriends screaming her head off.

"Look up at the sky, it'll seem more real," advises the nonchalant girl in her nonchalant tone.

The other mechanically complies, but soon interrupting her wailing lament—sincere this time—she's astonished to see that there's already a full moon, and that it's already up and shining at such an early hour.

"Is that normal?"

Turned on more by the earth than the sky, and less by heavenly bodies than the flesh and blood sort, the bubble-gum girl, instead of raising her eyes along with the others, exclaims "Hey, look! Grumps is back." Sure enough, the security guard has reappeared on the residential blacktop—which he presently examines with an air of disgust, mumbling strings of "they" and "those" and "them," into which he mixes the occasional "Koch's bacillus." The girls call out to him from the parking lot. They stick out their tongues, blatantly start drawing on dusty car hoods with their fingers, spitting their chewing gum out onto the ground . . . A lopsided chase ensues wherein the three lively little pests sprint around in all directions while the guard gesticulates uselessly, hardly budging. The more he curses, the harder they laugh, mocking his limp and his bald spot, the result of some old head surgery.

"Yo! Yo! Fat-so!" they call in choral sing-song, alternating high and low notes in a relentless refrain.

Their voices carry, but no one at Madame Fenerolo's seems to mind, much less notice the sounds coming from the cold, belonging as they do to so different a world, wholly unrelated to that inside the cozy apartment. Thus, low or high notes notwithstanding, the manager greets her visitors as if nothing were happening: "Sit down, have a seat"—and what would they like to drink? Cola, beer, fruit juice . . . ?

She's at home, on her turf. Instinctively, among her furnishings, she knows how large a step to take, how wide a gesture to make, skillful at keeping her balance however tight her skirt or high her heels. And yet, she stumbles.

"It's nothing," she protests instantly, while extending a hand to her ankle.

Then, whether putting on a new show of composure as a counter to the dubious grin and shady eye of the hulk with the comb, or else genuinely

157

eager to lay eyes on her packaged apparel, she goes over to the living-room table.

"So, let's have a look, shall we?"

"I'll handle it," says Tis-Jus, "let me do it."

But he doesn't move, as if to willfully defer the time to act in order not to blunt the effect of the words that announced his action. Next, the reverse: actions without words, all swift execution, the moving forward, the crouching down, the removal of adhesive tape strip by strip and the unfolding of kraft paper. Then, without getting up or moving aside: "There . . ."

The girls having eventually ceased their ritornello, and the guard his barking, a buffer zone of silence settles between the public space—pushed into the distance—and the living room, cut off now from the rest of humanity. Certainly, various reverberations—pedestrian bustle, car or air traffic—all continue to penetrate the room; but these rumblings, drones, or other sounds now all carry with them the idea of wilderness. And when, in a little while, rising from below, a lapping sound is heard, that of four tires moving in first gear, even this sound, however familiar, conjures up not so much the visitors' parking lot as those silted terrains where the leg sinks knee-deep: the shallows of some backwater, a path forged by a relentless procession, soaked by a monsoon; or the endlessly trampled shores of a river where zebra, buffalo, and other animals gather to quench their thirst in the brown water at set times.

Whether distracted by the noise of tires or by these imaginary fauna, Madame Fenerolo is slow to react to the sight of the package's contents—"Wonderful!" Likewise, commanded by Ti-Jus to submit to a final fitting, she decides to comply only after a moment's hesitation.

"Now . . . ? Well, all right."

Yet another moment passes, and now the hulk with the comb is alone. Roaming distractedly around the living room, he manhandles a bibelot in his path, or shatters it, puts a gash in a pillow cushion, beheads a plant, while in the bedroom Madame Fenerolo is taking offense: "What do you think you're . . . ?" Ti-Jus lifts her up. "I'm going to . . . !" she resists. Ti-Jus prevents her from saying anything further. She feels dizzy. She grasps at whatever she can, but bumps into the wall, the wardrobe, the bed frame; and when the world has stopped spinning around her, it bears down as a crushing weight on her plexus. She can't breathe. Her bones are dislocating, tissues tearing. She hurts, not knowing whether her arms and legs are still attached to her torso, whether what's cutting her is steal or fire, whether the blinding point of light toward which she feels herself hurtling is located inside her or is closing in from the outside, coming in for the kill.

In the hallway, leaning against the hummingbird-motif wallpaper, the hulk with the comb tips his head to one side. He blinks, while pointing an index finger in the direction of the bedroom—on the verge of saying what . . . ? Thinking again, however, and swinging his upper body insistently, as though this is enough to supplant speech, or even thought, he returns to the living room.

Outdoors, night has finally merged the various separate zones in the landscape that nevertheless appear in starker contrast than a while before, at sunset. The hulk recognizes the long trail of light that is Avenue de Paris, the red dots of the aerial beacons at Évry, the black sheet of woodland in Bas-de-Ris. He approaches the picture window. But he's only just pressed his palms against the glass when he jerks them back and steps away in a sudden reflex action, as if horrified by his icy contact with the vast open sky and the gloom-soaked suburb outside.

Situated though they are beneath that same vast openness, within that same chill and that same gloom, the young girls, on the contrary, seem quite at ease, settled down now among the cars in the parking lot. Whether the bubble-gum girl and her chum, tenderly entwined, or the nonchalant girl on a car hood, cheek to her knees, they appear delightfully drowsy, each pressed up against the night like a child to the mother's bosom—hearing both the mother's intimate voice and the noises of the world filtered; perceiving them at once within oneself and out in the world, perceiving oneself as a self in the world and the world as within oneself . . . Intermittently, one or the other of the three girlfriends starts softly humming some popular tune. Or a lethargic voice, seemingly half-asleep, complains—how much longer will they have to wait . . . ? Every now and then, a gum bubble bursts. Should the pink filaments stick to her lips, in a tone betraying the pleasure of the word more than serious annoyance or actual disgust, the little bubble-gum girl lets out a series of curses—*'zus christ, fucking mess, yuk,* or *plasmaph',* for *plasmaphele.*

PETROS ABATZOGLOU, *What Does Mrs. Freeman Want?*
MICHAL AJVAZ, *The Other City.*
PIERRE ALBERT-BIROT, *Grabinoulor.*
YUZ ALESHKOVSKY, *Kangaroo.*
FELIPE ALFAU, *Chromos.*
   Locos.
IVAN ÂNGELO, *The Celebration.*
   The Tower of Glass.
DAVID ANTIN, *Talking.*
ANTÓNIO LOBO ANTUNES, *Knowledge of Hell.*
ALAIN ARIAS-MISSON, *Theatre of Incest.*
JOHN ASHBERY AND JAMES SCHUYLER, *A Nest of Ninnies.*
DJUNA BARNES, *Ladies Almanack.*
   Ryder.
JOHN BARTH, *LETTERS.*
   Sabbatical.
DONALD BARTHELME, *The King.*
   Paradise.
SVETISLAV BASARA, *Chinese Letter.*
MARK BINELLI, *Sacco and Vanzetti Must Die!*
ANDREI BITOV, *Pushkin House.*
LOUIS PAUL BOON, *Chapel Road.*
   Summer in Termuren.
ROGER BOYLAN, *Killoyle.*
IGNÁCIO DE LOYOLA BRANDÃO, *Anonymous Celebrity.*
   Teeth under the Sun.
   Zero.
BONNIE BREMSER, *Troia: Mexican Memoirs.*
CHRISTINE BROOKE-ROSE, *Amalgamemnon.*
BRIGID BROPHY, *In Transit.*
MEREDITH BROSNAN, *Mr. Dynamite.*
GERALD L. BRUNS,
   Modern Poetry and the Idea of Language.
EVGENY BUNIMOVICH AND J. KATES, EDS.,
   Contemporary Russian Poetry: An Anthology.
GABRIELLE BURTON, *Heartbreak Hotel.*
MICHEL BUTOR, *Degrees.*
   Mobile.
   Portrait of the Artist as a Young Ape.
G. CABRERA INFANTE, *Infante's Inferno.*
   Three Trapped Tigers.
JULIETA CAMPOS, *The Fear of Losing Eurydice.*
ANNE CARSON, *Eros the Bittersweet.*
CAMILO JOSÉ CELA, *Christ versus Arizona.*
   The Family of Pascual Duarte.
   The Hive.
LOUIS-FERDINAND CÉLINE, *Castle to Castle.*
   Conversations with Professor Y.
   London Bridge.
   Normance.
   North.
   Rigadoon.
HUGO CHARTERIS, *The Tide Is Right.*
JEROME CHARYN, *The Tar Baby.*
MARC CHOLODENKO, *Mordechai Schamz.*
EMILY HOLMES COLEMAN, *The Shutter of Snow.*
ROBERT COOVER, *A Night at the Movies.*
STANLEY CRAWFORD, *Log of the S.S. The Mrs Unguentine.*
   Some Instructions to My Wife.
ROBERT CREELEY, *Collected Prose.*
RENÉ CREVEL, *Putting My Foot in It.*
RALPH CUSACK, *Cadenza.*
SUSAN DAITCH, *L.C.*
   Storytown.
NICHOLAS DELBANCO, *The Count of Concord.*
NIGEL DENNIS, *Cards of Identity.*
PETER DIMOCK,
   A Short Rhetoric for Leaving the Family.
ARIEL DORFMAN, *Konfidenz.*
COLEMAN DOWELL, *The Houses of Children.*
   Island People.
   Too Much Flesh and Jabez.
ARKADII DRAGOMOSHCHENKO, *Dust.*
RIKKI DUCORNET, *The Complete Butcher's Tales.*
   The Fountains of Neptune.
   The Jade Cabinet.
   The One Marvelous Thing.
   Phosphor in Dreamland.
   The Stain.
   The Word "Desire."
WILLIAM EASTLAKE, *The Bamboo Bed.*
   Castle Keep.
   Lyric of the Circle Heart.
JEAN ECHENOZ, *Chopin's Move.*
STANLEY ELKIN, *A Bad Man.*
   Boswell: A Modern Comedy.
   Criers and Kibitzers, Kibitzers and Criers.
   The Dick Gibson Show.
   The Franchiser.
   George Mills.
   The Living End.
   The MacGuffin.
   The Magic Kingdom.
   Mrs. Ted Bliss.
   The Rabbi of Lud.
   Van Gogh's Room at Arles.
ANNIE ERNAUX, *Cleaned Out.*
LAUREN FAIRBANKS, *Muzzle Thyself.*
   Sister Carrie.

JUAN FILLOY, *Op Oloop.*
LESLIE A. FIEDLER, *Love and Death in the American*
   Novel.
GUSTAVE FLAUBERT, *Bouvard and Pécuchet.*
KASS FLEISHER, *Talking out of School.*
FORD MADOX FORD, *The March of Literature.*
JON FOSSE, *Melancholy.*
MAX FRISCH, *I'm Not Stiller.*
   Man in the Holocene.
CARLOS FUENTES, *Christopher Unborn.*
   Distant Relations.
   Terra Nostra.
   Where the Air Is Clear.
JANICE GALLOWAY, *Foreign Parts.*
   The Trick Is to Keep Breathing.
WILLIAM H. GASS, *Cartesian Sonata and Other Novellas.*
   Finding a Form.
   A Temple of Texts.
   The Tunnel.
   Willie Masters' Lonesome Wife.
GÉRARD GAVARRY, *Hopla! 1 2 3.*
ETIENNE GILSON, *The Arts of the Beautiful.*
   Forms and Substances in the Arts.
C. S. GISCOMBE, *Giscome Road.*
   Here.
   Prairie Style.
DOUGLAS GLOVER, *Bad News of the Heart.*
   The Enamoured Knight.
WITOLD GOMBROWICZ, *A Kind of Testament.*
KAREN ELIZABETH GORDON, *The Red Shoes.*
GEORGI GOSPODINOV, *Natural Novel.*
JUAN GOYTISOLO, *Count Julian.*
   Juan the Landless.
   Makbara.
   Marks of Identity.
PATRICK GRAINVILLE, *The Cave of Heaven.*
HENRY GREEN, *Back.*
   Blindness.
   Concluding.
   Doting.
   Nothing.
JIŘÍ GRUŠA, *The Questionnaire.*
GABRIEL GUDDING, *Rhode Island Notebook.*
JOHN HAWKES, *Whistlejacket.*
AIDAN HIGGINS, *A Bestiary.*
   Bornholm Night-Ferry.
   Flotsam and Jetsam.
   Langrishe, Go Down.
   Scenes from a Receding Past.
   Windy Arbours.
ALDOUS HUXLEY, *Antic Hay.*
   Crome Yellow.
   Point Counter Point.
   Those Barren Leaves.
   Time Must Have a Stop.
MIKHAIL IOSSEL AND JEFF PARKER, EDS., *Amerika:*
   Contemporary Russians View the United States.
GERT JONKE, *Geometric Regional Novel.*
   Homage to Czerny.
JACQUES JOUET, *Mountain R.*
   Savage.
HUGH KENNER, *The Counterfeiters.*
   Flaubert, Joyce and Beckett: The Stoic Comedians.
   Joyce's Voices.
DANILO KIŠ, *Garden, Ashes.*
   A Tomb for Boris Davidovich.
ANITA KONKKA, *A Fool's Paradise.*
GEORGE KONRÁD, *The City Builder.*
TADEUSZ KONWICKI, *A Minor Apocalypse.*
   The Polish Complex.
MENIS KOUMANDAREAS, *Koula.*
ELAINE KRAF, *The Princess of 72nd Street.*
JIM KRUSOE, *Iceland.*
EWA KURYLUK, *Century 21.*
ERIC LAURRENT, *Do Not Touch.*
VIOLETTE LEDUC, *La Bâtarde.*
DEBORAH LEVY, *Billy and Girl.*
   Pillow Talk in Europe and Other Places.
JOSÉ LEZAMA LIMA, *Paradiso.*
ROSA LIKSOM, *Dark Paradise.*
OSMAN LINS, *Avalovara.*
   The Queen of the Prisons of Greece.
ALF MAC LOCHLAINN, *The Corpus in the Library.*
   Out of Focus.
RON LOEWINSOHN, *Magnetic Field(s).*
BRIAN LYNCH, *The Winner of Sorrow.*
D. KEITH MANO, *Take Five.*
MICHELINE AHARONIAN MARCOM, *The Mirror in the Well.*
BEN MARCUS, *The Age of Wire and String.*
WALLACE MARKFIELD, *Teitlebaum's Window.*
   To an Early Grave.
DAVID MARKSON, *Reader's Block.*
   Springer's Progress.
   Wittgenstein's Mistress.
CAROLE MASO, *AVA.*
LADISLAV MATEJKA AND KRYSTYNA POMORSKA, EDS.,
   Readings in Russian Poetics: Formalist and
   Structuralist Views.

FOR A FULL LIST OF PUBLICATIONS, VISIT:
www.dalkeyarchive.com

SELECTED DALKEY ARCHIVE PAPERBACKS

HARRY MATHEWS,
The Case of the Persevering Maltese: Collected Essays.
Cigarettes.
The Conversions.
The Human Country: New and Collected Stories.
The Journalist.
My Life in CIA.
Singular Pleasures.
The Sinking of the Odradek Stadium.
Tlooth.
20 Lines a Day.
ROBERT L. MCLAUGHLIN, ED.,
Innovations: An Anthology of Modern & Contemporary Fiction.
HERMAN MELVILLE, *The Confidence-Man.*
AMANDA MICHALOPOULOU, *I'd Like.*
STEVEN MILLHAUSER, *The Barnum Museum.*
In the Penny Arcade.
RALPH J. MILLS, JR., *Essays on Poetry.*
OLIVE MOORE, *Spleen.*
NICHOLAS MOSLEY, *Accident.*
Assassins.
Catastrophe Practice.
Children of Darkness and Light.
Experience and Religion.
God's Hazard.
The Hesperides Tree.
Hopeful Monsters.
Imago Bird.
Impossible Object.
Inventing God.
Judith.
Look at the Dark.
Natalie Natalia.
Paradoxes of Peace.
Serpent.
Time at War.
The Uses of Slime Mould: Essays of Four Decades.
WARREN MOTTE,
Fables of the Novel: French Fiction since 1990.
Fiction Now: The French Novel in the 21st Century.
Oulipo: A Primer of Potential Literature.
YVES NAVARRE, *Our Share of Time.*
Sweet Tooth.
DOROTHY NELSON, *In Night's City.*
Tar and Feathers.
WILFRIDO D. NOLLEDO, *But for the Lovers.*
FLANN O'BRIEN, *At Swim-Two-Birds.*
At War.
The Best of Myles.
The Dalkey Archive.
Further Cuttings.
The Hard Life.
The Poor Mouth.
The Third Policeman.
CLAUDE OLLIER, *The Mise-en-Scène.*
PATRIK OUŘEDNÍK, *Europeana.*
FERNANDO DEL PASO, *News from the Empire.*
Palinuro of Mexico.
ROBERT PINGET, *The Inquisitory.*
Mahu or The Material.
Trio.
MANUEL PUIG, *Betrayed by Rita Hayworth.*
RAYMOND QUENEAU, *The Last Days.*
Odile.
Pierrot Mon Ami.
Saint Glinglin.
ANN QUIN, *Berg.*
Passages.
Three.
Tripticks.
ISHMAEL REED, *The Free-Lance Pallbearers.*
The Last Days of Louisiana Red.
Reckless Eyeballing.
The Terrible Threes.
The Terrible Twos.
Yellow Back Radio Broke-Down.
JEAN RICARDOU, *Place Names.*
RAINER MARIA RILKE,
The Notebooks of Malte Laurids Brigge.
JULIÁN RÍOS, *Larva: A Midsummer Night's Babel.*
Poundemonium.
AUGUSTO ROA BASTOS, *I the Supreme.*
OLIVIER ROLIN, *Hotel Crystal.*
JACQUES ROUBAUD, *The Form of a City Changes Faster, Alas, Than the Human Heart.*
The Great Fire of London.
Hortense in Exile.
Hortense Is Abducted.
The Loop.
The Plurality of Worlds of Lewis.
The Princess Hoppy.
Some Thing Black.
LEON S. ROUDIEZ, *French Fiction Revisited.*

VEDRANA RUDAN, *Night.*
LYDIE SALVAYRE, *The Company of Ghosts.*
Everyday Life.
The Lecture.
The Power of Flies.
LUIS RAFAEL SÁNCHEZ, *Macho Camacho's Beat.*
SEVERO SARDUY, *Cobra & Maitreya.*
NATHALIE SARRAUTE, *Do You Hear Them?*
Martereau.
The Planetarium.
ARNO SCHMIDT, *Collected Stories.*
Nobodaddy's Children.
CHRISTINE SCHUTT, *Nightwork.*
GAIL SCOTT, *My Paris.*
DAMION SEARLS, *What We Were Doing and Where We Were Going.*
JUNE AKERS SEESE,
Is This What Other Women Feel Too?
What Waiting Really Means.
BERNARD SHARE, *Inish.*
Transit.
AURELIE SHEEHAN, *Jack Kerouac Is Pregnant.*
VIKTOR SHKLOVSKY, *Knight's Move.*
A Sentimental Journey: Memoirs 1917–1922.
Energy of Delusion: A Book on Plot.
Literature and Cinematography.
Theory of Prose.
Third Factory.
Zoo, or Letters Not about Love.
JOSEF ŠKVORECKÝ,
The Engineer of Human Souls.
CLAUDE SIMON, *The Invitation.*
GILBERT SORRENTINO, *Aberration of Starlight.*
Blue Pastoral.
Crystal Vision.
Imaginative Qualities of Actual Things.
Mulligan Stew.
Pack of Lies.
Red the Fiend.
The Sky Changes.
Something Said.
Splendide-Hôtel.
Steelwork.
Under the Shadow.
W. M. SPACKMAN, *The Complete Fiction.*
GERTRUDE STEIN, *Lucy Church Amiably.*
The Making of Americans.
A Novel of Thank You.
PIOTR SZEWC, *Annihilation.*
STEFAN THEMERSON, *Hobson's Island.*
The Mystery of the Sardine.
Tom Harris.
JEAN-PHILIPPE TOUSSAINT, *The Bathroom.*
Camera.
Monsieur.
Television.
DUMITRU TSEPENEAG, *Pigeon Post.*
The Necessary Marriage.
Vain Art of the Fugue.
ESTHER TUSQUETS, *Stranded.*
DUBRAVKA UGRESIC, *Lend Me Your Character.*
Thank You for Not Reading.
MATI UNT, *Brecht at Night*
Diary of a Blood Donor.
Things in the Night.
ÁLVARO URIBE AND OLIVIA SEARS, EDS.,
The Best of Contemporary Mexican Fiction.
ELOY URROZ, *The Obstacles.*
LUISA VALENZUELA, *He Who Searches.*
PAUL VERHAEGHEN, *Omega Minor.*
MARJA-LIISA VARTIO, *The Parson's Widow.*
BORIS VIAN, *Heartsnatcher.*
AUSTRYN WAINHOUSE, *Hedyphagetica.*
PAUL WEST, *Words for a Deaf Daughter & Gala.*
CURTIS WHITE, *America's Magic Mountain.*
The Idea of Home.
Memories of My Father Watching TV.
Monstrous Possibility: An Invitation to Literary Politics.
Requiem.
DIANE WILLIAMS, *Excitability: Selected Stories.*
Romancer Erector.
DOUGLAS WOOLF, *Wall to Wall.*
Ya! & John-Juan.
JAY WRIGHT, *Polynomials and Pollen.*
The Presentable Art of Reading Absence.
PHILIP WYLIE, *Generation of Vipers.*
MARGUERITE YOUNG, *Angel in the Forest.*
Miss MacIntosh, My Darling.
REYOUNG, *Unbabbling.*
ZORAN ŽIVKOVIĆ, *Hidden Camera.*
LOUIS ZUKOFSKY, *Collected Fiction.*
SCOTT ZWIREN, *God Head.*

FOR A FULL LIST OF PUBLICATIONS, VISIT:
www.dalkeyarchive.com